WILD HEARTS

SUITOR'S CROSSING: HEARTS COLLIDE

BOOK THREE

HALLIE BENNETT

I0619490

Searching for more obsessed heroes?
Check out the Mountain Men of
Suitor's Crossing series!

And don't miss out on Hallie Bennett updates by

joining her VIPs!

CHAPTER ONE

GRACE THOMPSON

The two-lane highway heading into Suitor's Crossing is deserted, and I pray civilization isn't too far away. My phone's GPS said it would be ten minutes before I reached my friend Elsie's apartment, but that was before my tire blew, leaving me stranded on the side of the road.

Walking is a whole other story.

Glancing up and down the empty road, all I see is a forest of trees—a sight I admired five minutes ago, especially as a Kansas plains native. Now? It looks like the beginning of a horror movie where the heroine gets lost in the woods before being chased by a man with a chainsaw.

Not today, Satan.

I didn't move across the country for a fresh start only to meet a grisly death. My luck isn't *that* bad, right?

A quick Google search shows a mechanic's shop called Dusty's located a mile away, and that's all I need to boost my spirits. "That's totally doable, right, boy?"

My dog wags his tail in agreement, creating a rhythmic thumping against the backseat. Shadow and I have been cooped up in the car for hours. It'll be good to stretch our legs, even if I'm not exactly dressed for a short hike.

"Come on! Looks like our adventure starts now." Shadow jumps out and waits as I grab my purse from the passenger's side floor and lock the car. "You really are a good dog, you know that?"

Shadow tilts his head as if to say, "I know, Mom."

Laughing at his sass, we begin our trek down the road. Like travelers of old, we'll arrive at our new home on foot, something I try to consider a good omen.

Suitor's Crossing represents a new beginning after a hellish couple of years stuck living with my family. Honestly, I feared ever escaping the hole I found myself in until Avery mentioned a job opening for a local firm, and things fell into place from there.

I packed my meager belongings in the car, then Shadow and I hit the road a day after the two weeks' notice at my previous job ended. Now, we're finally here... *sort of.*

Majestic pines guide our path on the gravel shoulder of the highway, camouflaging any signs of an actual town within its green depths. It's so different from my childhood on the prairie.

Don't get me wrong, Kansas has its own appeal with miles of fields as far as the eye can see and gentle rolling hills intermittently interrupting the flat landscape. But this sense of being cocooned by nature comforts my soul in a way the corn and wheat fields never did.

The weather is milder, too. Rather than the thirty-degree chill I left behind, it's a cool fifty degrees, perfect for showcasing my cute but warm outfit instead of hiding it beneath a puffy winter coat.

Another way I'm trying to branch out of my comfort zone.

In an attempt to dress the way I've always wanted to, instead of how people think a curvy girl like me should, high-waisted skinny jeans hug my wide hips and ass while an oversized red and black plaid shirt drapes over a tucked-in tank. Aside from the plaid shirt, everything conforms to my curves, and as someone who never considered tucking her shirts for fear of a muffin top, I'm proud to say I actually feel pretty.

Lumberjack chic.

I should blend right into the mountain town of Suitor's Crossing. Maybe even catch a mountain man.

One step at a time.

But the thought of finally having the time and mental capacity to fall in love is intoxicating. Life these past few years has drained me of the sort of energy necessary to maintain a relationship, so it's hard not to feel giddy at the prospect of being in a better mental space—one that could result in a loving relationship.

According to Avery, Suitor's Crossing is known for bringing couples together, too. There's an old landmark bridge the town is named after, where couples went "sparkin'" or what we'd consider "dating" these days, and *heart sparks* are a hallmark of the town.

Love at first sight.

It sounds so romantic and easy.

What I wouldn't give to meet a man, know he's the one, and for him to feel the same way about me. We could skip all the messy middle parts of second-guessing if it's right or not.

"Would you like a dog dad, Shadow?" Aside from my dad, he hasn't been around many men lately, so all he does is huff like he couldn't care less about the male species as long as he's got me.

Sweet boy.

And yes, I realize I may be a little bit of a crazy dog mom assigning meaning to his canine responses. That's what happens when your only close friend for nearly three years is a clingy German Shepherd.

Thirty minutes pass before a garage covered in peeling paint appears in front of us. The name matches the one on my phone, but that's the only point in its favor.

"Do you think they're open?"

Vehicles litter the front gravel area, but I don't see any people or an OPEN sign. However, this is the first glimpse of civilization we've seen, so I cross my fingers and approach the front entrance.

"The lights are on. That's promising," I say as I push the door open.

A little bell rings overhead, alerting whoever is working that someone entered. The pounding of loud bass reverberates from the back of the rundown waiting room. How anyone is supposed to hear that bell is a mystery to me, but I wait at the front counter anyway while Shadow explores the small space.

Looking for danger, I suppose. *Or just being a curious dog.* But I prefer to think the latter.

Shadow is a naturally protective German Shepherd, but he was also military-trained, though it's been years since he was in service. It took forever for me to get approved as his owner, but the mountain of paperwork and interviews were worth it. He makes me feel safe, which calms my anxious heart and mind.

Dust floats in the air, and a light film of it coats everything in the room. It's clear no one has cleaned in a while.

Who owns this place?

Some old man who's had it in his family for generations?

Someone too focused on cars to care about upkeep?

It was probably a super cute shop back in its prime, too. The decorations and furniture look to be original, just needing some TLC to bring them back to life again.

I bet his wife took care of that before she died.

As my mind starts spinning a tragic tale of poor Dusty's life, a younger man emerges from a back door. He's definitely not the sweet old-timer I was expecting.

"Shadow." Immediately, he comes to stand by my side, attuned to the wariness in my voice. I know it's not right to judge a book by its cover, but I'm a woman alone with a man who looks like he stepped out of a *Sons of Anarchy* episode, and a girl can never be too careful.

The stranger studies Shadow before spearing me with his dark gaze.

"Can I help you?" His gravelly voice perfectly matches my idea of him smoking and drinking on a daily basis. Habits I normally wouldn't find attractive in a man, but paired with his voice and rugged appearance, they suddenly seem extremely sexy.

What the hell? First, you're worried he might be dangerous, and now you think he's hot?

"Um... one of my car's tires exploded a little ways up the road. I was hoping someone could tow it and replace the tire." At least my voice doesn't reveal my inner turmoil. I sound completely normal.

"Did you walk here?" His brown eyes study me from head to toe until a grim line forms on his mouth.

Instinctively, my shoulders curl forward, and I cross my arms as if to protect myself from his unfavorable assessment.

Does he think I'm too fat to walk a freaking mile? The burgeoning attraction in my belly dampens at the possibility. Of course, he'd judge me.

You judged him first.

However true that may be, it still stings to learn parts of my past might follow me here, too. Like men not giving me a second glance.

Oh, sure, I wasn't in a place to accept a date back in Kansas, but the truth is no one ever asked. No one ever tested my resolve to stay single amid the drama of my family.

Guess my outfit isn't as cute as I thought.

"Yeah, but it wasn't too bad. It's pretty nice out for fall." I shrug, determined to remain composed, despite the insecurity threatening to take over. "Are you Dusty?"

The man clips a sheet of paper to a clipboard and snickers. "No, definitely not. Dusty owned this place long before it came into my possession, but his name stuck. I'm Wes." He hands the clipboard to me, and I note his finger tattoos—random symbols interspersed with black oil stains.

"Grace, and this is Shadow." I point the tip of the pen downward. Shadow must have deemed Wes safe enough, since he's sitting patiently by my side without a raised hackle in sight.

Wes nods and waits for me to finish completing the form before taking my car key. "Sit tight, and we'll get you fixed up. It shouldn't take too long."

"Thanks!" He doesn't return my smile, so it falters as he disappears back into the garage. Taking a seat by the window, I sigh. "Sorry about the minor freak out, boy." Shadow rests his head on my knee for pets, which I gladly give him.

It had been a shock seeing Wes in the place of old man Dusty. His rugged appearance screamed *I could break you if I want to.*

Not that he gave off those vibes in our conversation, but at first glance, my imagination went a little wild. His sleeves had been rolled up to reveal a myriad of tattoos lining his skin. No color, just black ink to match the tats on his fingers, his shoulder-length hair, and beard.

Honestly, I'm not sure if he's twenty-five or forty underneath everything, but his eyes hint at youth—ebony with a hint of laugh lines.

Although, Wes doesn't strike me as the kind of guy who laughs a lot. Maybe they're the start of glaring lines. Can you get eye wrinkles from intimidating glares?

"This mountain air might be making me a little loopy," I murmur because I can't stop dissecting my brief interaction with Wes. The anxiety windmills are spinning at full speed from his obvious disapproval of my appearance to the magnetic pull his bad boy persona has on me, despite knowing I'd never act on such an attraction. I may be turning over a new leaf—*or trying to*—but that doesn't mean I'm delusional enough to believe a man like Wes would be interested in a woman like me.

The thought is laughable.

Texting Elsie and Avery about the current situation, they offer to pick me up so I don't have to hang out here. I probably should've texted them the moment my car rattled to the side of the road, but the exercise was good for me. And now they can give me a brief tour of the town before I need to pick up my fixed car.

And you can fill your head with something other than the mechanic who is a dark Charlie Hunnam look-alike.

CHAPTER TWO

WES GALLAGHER

Laughter hangs in the air as I enter the waiting room, scrubbing away the grease on my hands with a ragged hand towel. Alex is kneeling on the floor and petting a familiar German Shepherd while flirting with its owner—the pretty stranger, Grace Thompson.

Typical.

"I don't pay you to fucking flirt, Alex." The growled words cause Grace to jump in surprise, her skin flushing red as she brushes a loose curl off her cheek.

Dammit, I didn't mean to scare her.

Attempting a more civil tone, I add, "Get back to work. I'll handle this."

Alex waves goodbye to Grace with a wink before muttering under his breath, "Whatever you say, boss man," and the sarcastic note in his voice grates on my nerves.

We were friendly acquaintances before I hired him to work at Dusty's, but he needs to learn to respect me at work. Otherwise, our friendship, and his position, will be in jeopardy. Because I don't tolerate attitude from those working for me. I get enough of that from certain townspeople already.

Forcing the issue of Alex aside, I focus on Grace and admire the thick thighs encased in her skintight jeans before dropping to her trim ankles covered by suede. I still can't believe she hiked here in those boots. She's lucky if blisters don't form from the long trek.

"Everything should be fine now. We replaced your tire and inspected the rest of the vehicle to double-check everything else."

Because I couldn't resist ensuring it was safe for her to drive.

Because, for some reason, I feel protective of Grace.

You barely fucking know the woman. Not to mention you don't do relationships.

And ensuring a car's safety beyond what's necessary?

Seems like the kind of thing a man does for his woman.

After collecting payment, I gesture out the window to where her car is parked. "Your keys are in the driver's seat. If you need anything else, give us a call." Maybe if I hustle Grace out the door, my mind will stop wandering to images of those thighs wrapped around my shoulders as I eat her out on the hood of my truck.

Fuck.

It's obvious I need to get laid if a customer is affecting me this way. I never mix business with pleasure, although technically, I suppose our business is done...

"Thank you so much! I really appreciate how quickly you fit me in and finished everything." Her face brightens with a blinding smile, distracting me from my wayward thoughts.

Damn, she's like a ray of fucking sunshine.

"Just doing my job." Uncomfortable with her gratitude for something I would've gladly done no matter how busy we were—and no, I'm not about to analyze the reason why—I broach the topic that's been on my mind since she walked into my shop. "Are you just passing through, or visiting someone in town?"

I would remember if I'd seen her around Suitor's Crossing before, so this is definitely her first visit. But how long will it last?

Grace opens the car door to let Shadow jump into the backseat after I walk her outside. "I'm actually moving here. My friends Elsie and Avery live in town and helped me get a job at Casey & Sons."

Fuck Casey.

My usual rejoinder to hearing about those douchebags resounds in my head, and I bite my tongue to keep it there. The Casey family thinks they're hot shit because they're one of the original inhabitants of Suitor's Crossing—at least, I assume the entire family is full of pretentious pricks to match the two younger sons. The twins, Andrew and Brandon Casey, and I attended the same schools from elementary to high school, so I witnessed them evolve from class nuisances to first-class bastards.

I hate that Grace will be working with them.

Jealous they'll get to see her every day.

You don't get jealous over women, remember?

"Congratulations," I grit out, fighting to remain neutral in the face of the conflicting emotions suddenly bombarding me. "Elsie... Do you mean Elsie Hawkins? A teacher at Scott Key Elementary? Had a dust-up with a parent last year?"

Could there be more than one Elsie in Suitor's Crossing? Sure, we're not *that* tiny, but we're also a town of magical coincidences, so it wouldn't surprise me if the one Elsie I'm aware of is Grace's friend.

Her blue eyes widened, and it's obvious I guessed correctly. Gossip is hard to miss in Suitor's Crossing, even for a guy like me—someone with a record that people tend to avoid. And a tale like Elsie's? One that includes Sheriff Lawson's ex-wife? Well, there was no way that wasn't spreading like wildfire to where I reside at the very edge of town.

"This really is a small town, huh?"

"You have no idea." A small town with a big attitude. At least towards those it deems unworthy of their esteem. *Like me.* Sure, we've got Hallmark charm with a bustling Main Street and events scheduled for practically every holiday, but everything—*and everyone*—ain't always sweet as a gumdrop.

"Guess that means we'll probably see each other around." Grace chuckles before settling in the driver's seat. "Thanks again for fixing my car. Have a good day!"

Right, we can't stand outside all day chitchatting. I've got work to do, and she's got a new life to start in town.

Her car disappears around the bend, and despite her optimistic remark, I doubt we'll see much of each other at all. Elsie runs in a certain circle of Suitor's Crossing, one I'm not a part of. Not that she's ever been anything but friendly towards me, but our paths don't often cross.

Which means mine and Grace's won't either.

It shouldn't bother me.

But damn if her sweet honey scent doesn't linger in Dusty's waiting room and make me wish I had more time with her.

IT'S NEVER GOOD WHEN my mom calls, so when her name appears on my phone an hour later, I immediately ignore it. We have a dislike/hate relationship—I dislike her, and she hates me.

"What?"

"Is that any way to greet your mother?" I don't respond to her comment, and she huffs on the other end of the line. "Are you planning to come home for Thanksgiving? Your brother would like to see you."

Step-brother.

He's from my mom's second marriage after she had enough of slumming it with my dad, a truck driver on the road ninety-percent of the time.

Jordan is a decent kid, which I can only attribute to his father's influence, but there's no way he enlisted our mom to invite me to Thanksgiving.

The last time I went to their house—because that's not my home—was for Jordan's sixteenth birthday in February.

"I'll let you know."

"Make sure you're here, Wesley. I don't know what Jordan sees in you, but you'll be a big disappointment if you don't show."

"I thought I already was one, Mother."

She snickers. "Yeah, well, your sweet brother hasn't learned yet." With that snide remark, the call ends, and I shove the phone back into my pocket with a curse.

And that's why I've never been interested in relationships.

My mom grew up in an upper middle-class family before falling for my dad in high school and 'downgrading'—her description, not mine.

Frankly, lust seems more likely than love, but either way, my parents ended up together and had me at the ripe old age of eighteen. Even as a kid, I recognized how different my mom and dad were from each other, and when Mom packed her belongings and hightailed it out of the trailer park? Well, I can't say I was surprised.

Doesn't mean it didn't sting like a motherfucker those first few years.

Until it became obvious how selfish she was on the rare times she deigned to visit me.

Then I got smart and vowed to never let another woman fuck around with my heart again.

CHAPTER THREE

GRACE

After a week of settling into Suitor's Crossing, I'm in love with the cozy little town. People are friendly, including my boss Jack Casey, Sr., which is a welcome change from my last job. My measly belongings are unpacked in the apartment I'm sharing with Elsie now that Avery moved in with her fiancé, and it feels like life is affirming my decision to start over here.

Which includes my plans for tonight.

On cue, my phone vibrates with a text from Kayla saying she's waiting for me outside, and I hurry to finish getting ready. Kayla is married to Mr. Casey's son, Brandon, and when she asked me to join her for a girls' night, I couldn't refuse the opportunity to make friends.

Because, let's face it, socializing is not my strong suit. I've never been brave enough to approach strangers and strike up a conversation. That's why Elsie, Avery, and I are so close—we're three peas in a pod. Although Avery has emerged from her hermit shell since meeting Dominic.

But this move is meant to help me become who I've always wanted to be—a woman who ventures out of her comfort zone to experience new things.

A woman who puts herself out there.

The only downside to this evening is that Elsie and Avery can't make it. Because while I talk a big game about change, I'd still like the security blanket of my best friends.

After double-checking myself in the bathroom mirror, I grab a jacket, pet Shadow goodbye, and head outside to Kayla's idling vehicle. I'm not sure where we're headed, but I figure I'll be safe in dark jeans and a dressy navy tank with a silver zipper down the front. My hair rests loose and wild over my shoulders, since I gave up trying to tame the curls a long time ago.

"Hey!" Kayla greets me as soon as I open the side door of a gold Suburban. "This is Brittany and Lindsey. Girls, this is Grace. She works with Brandon."

I slide into the backseat and smile at the two women. They ask the basic questions of where I'm from and why I moved before reverting to their previous conversation: some spat with another mother on the PTA.

Settling into the leather seat, my attention splits between listening to their conversation and counting to ten over and over again to calm my nerves. It's been a while since I've hung out with people I don't know extremely well, and the unknown expectations are already starting to get to me.

"Before we show you the best spots around town, we're gonna show you the worst, so you know what to avoid," Kayla says as she turns into a crowded parking lot. "Welcome to The Ole Aces."

"Home of dirty drunks and filthy bikers who may or may not have done time in prison," Brittany chimes in.

"But they definitely have." Kayla smirks, meeting my gaze in the rearview mirror.

Um, what?

"If these guys are dangerous, why are we hanging out here?" Seems like a no-brainer to avoid this place. A warning would have been sufficient, and we could have skipped this whole scene.

Bars have never been my thing, anyway.

I was secretly hoping for a nice dinner out on Main Street. *Stop being a coward. It hasn't worked for you so far.*

"Oh, they know better than to mess with one of us. Brandon's dad is a big name around here. The Casey family helped found Suitor's Crossing. They may have even originated the *heart sparks* legend."

A rundown of my bosses' background is unexpected and a little intimidating. I had no idea the Caseys were so influential. Avery hadn't mentioned it after redecorating the law firm's offices.

"Looks like a lot of Reaper's Wolves guys are here tonight," Brittany says, nodding ahead. Except for a gap allowing people access to the entrance, a line of gleaming motorcycles form a barricade in front of the bar.

The women's warnings have me braced for the overwhelming stench of alcohol and sweaty bodies packed into a dilapidated barroom, but the inside of The Ole Aces is anything but trashy or disgusting.

Couples two-step around a crowded dance floor while high tops and booths house groups of friends laughing and drinking. Country music blares from a sound system, causing me to wince at the noise—my eardrums will be cursing me by the end of the night—but other than the loud music, this seems like a fun place to hang out.

Wrought iron light fixtures add a modern feel to the rustic appeal, and it could be mistaken for a popular bar in any metropolis around the country.

"Here's a good spot!" Lindsey snags the last empty table along a wall in the back while my mind struggles to connect *this* Ole Aces with the one they described. We take our seats, though I'm far from relaxing, sitting ramrod straight in the high back chair.

Now is the time for small talk, and my flustered nerves are already shot. Especially since I'm not sure what I have in common with Kayla, Lindsey, and Brittany.

I'm not a mom, so the PTA is out.

And I'm not one of the country club set who sticks their noses up at a bar like The Ole Aces.

Suddenly, the welcoming embrace I received from them is reminiscent of a snake's chokehold.

Maybe I should have turned down Kayla's invitation, in favor of getting to know her casually at work first. Because now if things don't work out, my new job could become a very uncomfortable place. Kayla doesn't work at Casey & Sons, but she stops by frequently to see Brandon, which is how our paths crossed in the first place.

Either way, you were probably screwed. Kind of rude to turn down an invite from the boss's wife.

"The fun part is pretending you're watching a reality TV show. I bet we see two brawls and someone giving an MC member a handy on the dance floor. Tonight is the weekly line dancing event, so it's bound to get rowdy with people coming from High Ridge, too." Kayla sniffs in disdain.

The allure of coming here to diss the bar's patrons is lost on me. If this is how they choose to spend their Friday night, what's the big deal?

A man slips his hand up a woman's shirt at the edge of the dance floor, and snarky remarks erupt between Kayla, Lindsey, and Brittany.

"Alright, time to spice up our viewing party, we need alcohol! Since you're the new girl, round one is on you!" Lindsey points to me with glee.

Great.

As silly as it sounds, this is only my third time in a bar, and I've never been in one like this. My friends and I are coffee shop/book club people. The few bars we went to would be considered sedate compared to this place.

Grabbing my wristlet wallet, I make my way to the bar counter where two women and a guy are busy doling out a parade of drinks. I search for an opening but keep getting jostled back as others push to the front.

Suck it up, Grace. You're getting nowhere.

Gathering my courage, I shove my way forward as politely as possible until I catch the attention of one of the women. "Six shots of tequila, please."

Nice and simple. Who doesn't like tequila?

"Aren't you sweet? Hey, Jules, did you hear that? She said *please*!"

Jules laughs from her position filling pitchers of beer. I can't tell if she's genuinely thankful or sarcastic. Guess politeness doesn't get you very far here.

Being run over like an invisible mouse by other patrons should've been your first clue.

"Here you go, hun."

I pay and, with a nod of gratitude, attempt to beeline back to our table while balancing a tray full of shot glasses, but the small space I'd carved out on my way to the bar has been swallowed up again by a barrage of men. Somehow, I don't think they'd appreciate a *please* either.

Come on, you can do it. Stop being a mouse and move!

Head down, I weave a path through the crowd until a hand squeezes my butt. One jerk of surprise later, glass shatters as the fumbled shots hit the floor, and alcohol soaks my chest and stomach.

"Don't." A harsh voice growls behind me.

Is that...?

I spin around to confirm my suspicion. Wes has a hand around my perpetrator's arm, his eyes intense with a death glare.

Yep, that is definitely how he's getting those lines.

The overly handsy man shakes Wes off and retreats without a word. Probably because Wes is double his size and looks mad enough to draw blood. Unlike me, who clearly looked like an easy target.

"Thanks." My voice is barely above a whisper as I bend to pick up the broken glass.

"Leave it." He stops me with a hand on my shoulder, and I immediately move away, causing his arm to fall back to his side.

I know he's not trying anything, but I'm not used to being touched.

Let alone going from a stranger harassing me to the tingly spark Wes's rough palm on my skin elicited.

"You could cut yourself. Jules or somebody will sweep it up safely." His broad shoulders shrug in explanation as he continues to study me. He's wearing another black tee like the first time I saw him, and his beard is a little fuller like he's gone a few extra days without a shave.

Can't say it's a bad look.

Ignoring the electricity his undivided attention evokes, I focus on wiping the tequila off my arms. It's a sticky mess.

Twenty minutes into my first attempt at a new me, and I'm ready to head home, shower, and forget this night even happened. Kayla and I aren't on the fast track to becoming best buds. The agonizing I did over what to wear was for nothing since I'm soaked in alcohol. And to top it all off, the only attention I grabbed belonged to a pervert.

And Wes.

But really it wasn't me *personally* that drew him to step in. He probably would have defended any woman being bothered by a touchy creep.

"Look, Austin, the bar owner, has a room in the back with a sink and paper towels, so you can clean up." He gestures to a hallway where a sign for restrooms hangs overhead.

"Um... no, thanks... I'm g-good." I brush off the offer, too wired to be alone with him. My nerves are a frayed mess, and Wes coming to my rescue like a tattooed knight in shining armor already has me feeling tongue-tied.

"Seriously? I can see the drops of tequila on your skin, and unless you're planning on letting me take shots off you..." His voice trails off suggestively, his sable gaze a palpable caress over my body before zeroing in on my chest—specifically, the tight nipples poking through the cold fabric of my tank.

Flustered, I quickly cross my arms to hide them as my mind shuts off—fried from overload—and I squeak out something about needing to get back to my friends, whipping around to escape like the true mouse I am.

Wes was flirting with me.

That's what that was, right? But why?

I definitely don't seem like his type.

In a fitted shirt outlining his hard muscles, tattoos galore, and a *don't fuck with me* attitude, he fits in with The Ole Aces crowd.

I don't.

I'm too quiet, too strait-laced, even if I'm trying to be more outgoing. Even if his—*interested?*—gaze made my thighs clench in instant arousal.

"Hey, you forgot something."

"Hmm...?" Distracted by thoughts of Wes, I didn't realize I arrived back to our table—empty handed. Someone else is going to have to buy the next round of drinks, though, because I'm not braving the floor again.

A quick explanation of what went down tumbles out in one breathless go.

"You were right to refuse him. Wes Gallagher has a reputation around here," Kayla pauses knowingly. "Sleeps around. Gets in fights. He's even spent time in jail."

"Same as in high school," Brittany adds.

"You guys went to school together?" That answers my age question. Sneaking a peek towards the bar, I do the math to figure out he's only a few years older than me.

"Yep, and he's even worse now. I mean, look at him. We have our fair share of unkempt mountain men around here, but Wes looks like a fucking grizzly bear with the beard and long hair. Plus, he's friends with the Reaper's Wolves MC—a legitimate gang." Kayla leans back with a raised brow as if to say she rests her case.

A couple of bikers have cruised through town with leather cuts proclaiming their MC, so it doesn't surprise me that Wes knows them. He owns a body shop. They own motorcycles that require maintenance. It's not exactly a leap to connect the two.

Don't forget he looks like a raven-haired Charlie Hunnam, too—circa Sons of Anarchy.

Kayla taps a manicured finger on the table. "Trust us. Wes Gallagher is bad news. Born on the wrong side of town, he's never done anything to prove he's more than just white trash."

My gut tightens at the harsh label—a label I wouldn't be surprised to hear people call my family back home.

It's becoming increasingly clear that no matter how hopeful I was about tonight, Kayla and her crew wouldn't accept me if they knew my background. And, frankly, I'm not so desperate for friends that I'd condone their catty behavior.

I can be the new, outgoing me with Elsie and Avery. They've been enough for years, and they're still enough. Why do I need a larger support system anyway?

"He owns a business, though. Doesn't that count for something?" I'm not one for confrontation, but I hate the idea of being so weak that I can't defend someone who deserves it.

They all laugh at my statement. "How did you find that out? *Dusty's*," Lindsey shudders at the name, "is some dingy old building where he and his friends hang out. I can't imagine that place earns a profit. He didn't go to college, doesn't know the first thing about running a successful business."

"It looked like he was doing fine when I was there. Sure, it could use some..." I stop when their fascinated horror registers.

"You've been there? Why the hell would you do that?"

"She didn't know better at the time, obviously." Kayla rolls her eyes, flipping her highlighted hair over a shoulder. "Ugh, this is boring. Can we stop wasting our time discussing Wes Gallagher? He's not worth it."

I wholeheartedly agree with the decision to end this line of conversation. It's unfair to keep insulting him when he can't defend himself, and their judgment hits too close to home. Like I'll be next if they discover my family's drama and financial troubles.

My gaze finds Wes again, a strange bond with the man twisting in my belly.

Looks like we've got something in common, after all.

CHAPTER FOUR

WES

The Ole Aces is crowded for another wild Friday night. Most of the men and women just got paid, so everyone's itching to blow it all on a good time—except for me. I take another long drink from my beer as I survey the familiar faces, consciously avoiding the table of women to my far left.

Max bumps my shoulder with a wolfish grin. "What's it gonna be: blonde, brunette, ginger?"

Shaking my head, I refuse to answer. Max always tries to guess who I'll be taking home for the night. The problem is that none of the women here interest me. Most of them I've already fucked, while the rest are too damn annoying or bitchy.

Except for her.

My gaze wanders around the room again, allowing myself to briefly study Grace before moving on as if her curvy little body and shy demeanor haven't completely captured my attention.

"There's Lyssa. An oldie but a goodie?"

"Shut the fuck up." He damn well knows I'm done with Lyssa. We fucked a few times, but she kept desperately grasping for more. Acted like she owned me when no one did or ever would.

Max grins, flips me off, then returns to dance with his wife, Kendra.

I still can't believe he got married. And to a gem like Kendra Thurman.

Max used to be like me—a *fuck'em and leave'em* kind of guy. We loved our freedom, vowing to never chain ourselves to one woman for life.

Until Kendra moved back to Suitor's Crossing.

All of a sudden, the myths surrounding Suitor's Crossing about *heart sparks* and soulmates came true, because Max fell quickly, and he fell hard. Not that I begrudge his happiness, but sometimes I miss the way things used to be.

Damn, I'm fucking maudlin tonight.

I should be out on the floor locking down a woman to relieve the stress of another work week, but my mind and body refuse to rally any interest in what they'll find there.

Because of Grace.

When that cocky fuck reached out to touch her a second time, I'd instinctively stepped forward to stop him, a rush of fury filling my veins, and it confused the hell out of me.

I don't get overprotective or possessive of women.

I don't get jealous.

But all of those emotions rose to the forefront in an unprecedented crash, and I found myself defending Grace before I really had a moment to question why. I mean, I don't care to watch women get harassed, but this was more than a simple *leave her alone.*

Grace wasn't some nameless woman; I wasn't an objective bystander.

Far from it.

Then she'd immediately jerked away from my touch afterward, and that fucking stung. Nothing good can come from this damn fixation of mine. Hell, she couldn't even spend five minutes alone with me to clean up.

Women like Grace don't sully themselves with men like me—rough and uncouth.

Especially not after my comment about taking shots off her delectable body. That mistake sent her scampering back to the bitch squad led by Kayla. I can imagine the tales she's sharing with Grace.

Max and Kendra return to the bartop, and he follows my line of sight. "So... brunette?"

Not in this lifetime.

MY ALARM GOES OFF AT 6:15 AM the next morning for my daily run. Tossing on a pair of jogging shorts and a hoodie, I start stretching while mentally reviewing the list of errands for today—a roadmap to completing much-needed repairs on my house.

Due to its age and bad condition, I bought it for cheap a few months ago because I was tired of living in the small apartment above Dusty's. Always reeking of motor oil and tiny enough to be called a sardine box by Max, a change was necessary.

Purchasing a fixer-upper wasn't exactly what I had in mind, but I'm not afraid of hard work or learning new skills. Aware of my limits, I hired a crew to replace the roof first, then Max, a couple of Reaper's Wolves guys, and I worked on my bedroom and bathroom. Now we're on to the kitchen, where hopefully I'll finish the backsplash today.

The agenda set in my mind, I jog down the road, following my usual route. I love running at this time of day because it's quiet and empty of people, allowing me space to actually think.

Turning the corner towards Oak Park, my thoughts wander like the winding trails that lead through dense tree cover and over streams. The famous Suitor's Crossing bridge appears on my right, and like always, I avoid crossing it. Call me superstitious, but I don't need any chance of *heart sparks* sinking their claws into me.

I've evaded their clutches for three damn decades, so clearly I've gotten pretty good at dodging fate or whatever the hell is at work in this town.

An outcropping of rocks leads to a blind curve, which is when a cyclist rams into me from the other direction. My back hits the ground as an expletive echoes through the peaceful forest.

"Goddamn! Ever hear of watching for pedestrians?"

A growling dog jumps into view, teeth bared, black and tan hackles raised and oddly familiar.

"Shadow, *komm*!" Although the German command comes through labored breathing, the dog retreats to its owner's side. *Grace's* side. Her legs are tangled with a purple bike on the mulched path. "Sorry... Didn't see you." Shallow breaths puff from her chest as she remains flat on her back.

Anger forgotten, I crawl over to her, careful to seem non-threatening to Shadow as I disengage her from the fallen bike.

"Are you okay?" I survey her prone body and note the cuts on her palms and forearms, along with one long gash slicing up her calf.

"I'm f-fine... Just need... to catch my breath." Grace slowly pushes herself into a sitting position. We stare at each other in silence before she licks her lips and asks, "Do you always respond to accidents by yelling?"

I duck my head in embarrassment. "Unfortunately, yes. Sorry."

The apology feels foreign on my tongue. I don't apologize for my actions. I do what I want and *fuck you* if you have a problem with it.

Grace grimaces then gently pats along the back of her head. When she pulls her fingers away from her scalp, they're covered in blood.

"Oh, look, I'm bleeding..."

"Shit!" I rip off my hoodie and tee.

"W-what are you doing?" Her curious gaze roams over my bare chest and shoulders. She seems more concerned with my undressing than the blood gushing from her head, which can't be good.

How hard did she hit her head?

"Trying to help you."

"Getting naked is considered help?"

A reluctant chuckle rolls out of me. "When I need something to bandage an injured woman? Yes. Now, hold still." I tear a few strips off my shirt and wrap it around her head. The light fabric quickly darkens from the incessant bleeding. "Damn, this isn't working. We need to get you to the hospital."

"No!" The outburst shocks me with its vehemence. "No doctors. I just need to go home." She tries to stand, but I stop her.

"You can't go home yet. You probably need stitches."

Grace rolls her eyes. "You didn't even check to see how deep the cut is. Head wounds always bleed a lot. It seems worse than it is."

"You're kidding, right?"

"Can you grab my bike, please?"

"Hell, no. So, you can injure yourself even more?" Ignoring me, she stubbornly staggers to her feet, and I brace myself, ready to catch her as she lifts the bike with a groan.

"See, I'm fine. I didn't lose consciousness after the fall, so there's nothing to worry about." She bites her lip as if she's trying to convince herself as much as me. "I'll just walk home."

"You're really going to try and walk this off?" I study her pale complexion and the tight grip she has on the handlebars. She's trying to put up a good front but failing miserably. "You look like you're about to keel over any moment." Pulling out my phone, I call Max. He should be up by now since he's opening the shop.

"If you're calling 911, you're wasting your time."

"Relax, I'm calling us a ride." Once Max answers, I explain the situation and ask him to pick us up at the park. "Okay, my friend Max will be here in about ten minutes, which means you can sit now."

Grace hesitates like she's going to disobey the order then sinks down on a bench a few feet down the path.

"Finally, you listen. Was that so hard?" I grouse, lowering to a seat beside her, while Shadow stands sentinel between us until Max shows up. He shoots Grace a questioning look, her bandaged headdress dyed to different shades of pink and red at this point, but he keeps his mouth shut.

Wise man.

The two of us help Grace to his truck at the end of the trail—Max rolling her bike while I keep an arm wrapped around her soft waist. Shadow trots beside us, keeping a steady eye on the strangers near his mom.

"Alright, where am I going?"

Grace gives directions once we're in the truck cab. It's a five-minute drive to her apartment, and Max chatters the entire way. A barrage of questions are waiting for me at the end of this, since there's no way he doesn't recognize her as the woman from The Ole Aces last night.

But hell if I know how to answer them beyond laying out the facts of our accidental meeting this morning.

Grace smiles as Max cracks another joke, the first positive expression from her today, and it bugs the hell out of me that I'm not the one earning her favor.

Don't be an idiot. What's it matter?

After we're parked, I reach up to help Grace from the tall truck cab, but as my hands settle on her hips, she rears back. "What are you doing?"

The anxiety in her tone gives me pause. "Helping you down. You're short, and with a head injury, I don't think you should be jumping anytime soon."

Explanation tossed out, I take her in my arms, however unwillingly, and her nails find purchase in my shoulders as I gently lower her to the ground. The addicting scent of honey tickles my nose, tempting me to search out its source. Her hair? Her skin?

As soon as Grace's feet touch the graveled lot, she attempts to escape my hold, slamming me back to reality—a reality that's reinforced when she sways into the side of the truck.

"Whoa! I knew we should've taken you to the hospital." My arm curls protectively around her waist to steady her. "Come on. Let's get you inside."

Shadow trails us, keeping a close eye on me. I thank Max for the ride and send him back to work without a backward glance. I can jog home from here, and his inquisition can wait.

Once we enter the tiny apartment, I guide Grace to a beige and green couch before figuring out where the first aid kit is and gathering supplies for her wound.

"Moment of truth," I say as I sit next to her. "Let's see how bad this cut really is."

"You don't have to stay. I can take it from here."

"Nice try, but I'm not leaving until it's clear you're okay." The cut is underneath her ponytail, and I have her hold it to the side so I can see better. "Do you have a headache or anything?"

I remove the makeshift bandage, carefully separating the thin cloth from the riot of curls stuck to it.

"Not really. I'm a little tired, but that's probably because it's still early."

She's right. It's only 7:30. Everything happened so quickly.

"Or you have a concussion." I dab at the dried blood with a wet cloth from the kitchen until the wound becomes visible. "You'll probably have a scar, but I don't think it needs stitches since it stopped bleeding."

"That's a relief."

I hum in agreement, cleaning her up a little better. Red stains her neck and shirt—a little more blood and she could give *Carrie* a run for her money. "I'm no doctor, but I think we should leave this open to heal since I can't exactly put a bandage over your hair... Unless you'd consider shaving?" I tease before moving on to her other scrapes.

Grace snorts. "I'm not the one who needs a haircut."

"What's that supposed to mean?" I glance up to find her cheeks flushed.

"Nevermind. Thanks for... this." The last is hissed out as she flinches from the sting of alcohol.

"Sorry," I murmur, blowing gently over the spot. "Come on, tell me. You don't approve of my look?"

"Oh, no, I didn't mean to imply..." she stammers, shrugging her shoulders. "Your look kind of says... um... mountain man? But not in a bad way. I shouldn't have said anything. Kayla's diatribe must've gotten in my head."

"Kayla Casey? What else did she say about me?" No surprise that bitch is still trying to fuck with me.

"Nothing, really... I'm sorry I brought it up. It's your body. You can do what you want."

"Did she tell you how I refused her when she showed up at my home, naked beneath a trenchcoat? Like a cringey scene out of the movies." Grace's expression reflects her shock. "And that was just last month. She's been panting after me since high school."

"Last month? But she's married." Confusion laces her words, and a harsh bark of laughter rumbles from my chest.

"Married? Who fucking cares? Vows mean nothing to her. I'm pretty sure she and Brandon have fucked around on each other for years now."

Judging by the stunned look on her face, the news doesn't sit well, but if Kayla is going to slander my name, the least I can do in return is share the truth.

"I think you should go now," Grace whispers.

"Why? Because I shattered your illusion of perfect fucking Kayla?"

"No." She shifts to a single chair across from the couch. Shadow sits in front of her and rests his head on her lap. "Because I suffered a head injury and want to be alone."

Fuck. Thinking about that bitch Kayla had me completely forgetting the whole reason I'm here. Another apology falls from my lips, and I can't help but wonder what it is about this girl that's had me issue two apologies within the hour.

"Are you sure you should be alone? I can stay." I don't know why I'm offering. I know she'll turn me down, especially after my frustration with Kayla's lies got the best of me. But an idiotic part of my brain hopes Grace won't make me leave. That she'll see I'm not the loser Kayla and her posse painted me to be.

"I'm sure. I've got Shadow if anything happens, which it won't. Plus, my roommate Elsie should be home soon from this breakfast thing she had to attend. Thanks again for everything, and I'm sorry for hitting you with my bike."

Dismissed.

It's obvious I'm no longer welcome.

Hell, that's the story of my life.

Doesn't stop me from making one last promise, though. "If you need anything, call Dusty's and ask for me. I'll be here." Then I finally leave.

CHAPTER FIVE

GRACE

O nce Wes leaves, most of my cool deserts me as I grab my phone and send a frantic text to the group chat with Elsie and Avery.

"What a morning, huh, Shadow?" He looks at me with his intelligent golden eyes. The whole time with Wes, he'd been on guard. Not quite threatened but wary of a man in his home. "You did great today."

He listened when I told him to come, using the German command like I was taught, and eased my anxiety with the two men. Not that I feared them, but it's not often that I'm alone and injured with strangers, so it's better to be safe than sorry. I scratch Shadow's pointed ears as I gaze out my front window, recalling the whirlwind morning events.

Wes tearing off his clothes to reveal a tattooed chest sprinkled with wiry hair.

The strength of his muscled body as he hauled me out of Max's truck.

Me insulting his beard and shaggy hair with the 'mountain man' comment.

"You're lucky you can't say dumb shit like that, Shadow." It was the first thing that came to mind after blurting out the nonsense about a haircut.

Something he doesn't even need.

Because *mountain man* or *grizzly bear* like Kayla said, he's hot and rugged, and the combination sends my hormones into a frenzy whenever he's near. A reaction that sucks since it turns me into a stuttering mess who struggles to have a conversation with the man.

There were so many silences today.

First, because I couldn't breathe due to the accident, and then, because any interesting thought I'd ever had evaporated under the heat of his presence.

Did that magically stop me from humiliating myself by insulting him, though? *Of course not.*

My phone rings with a call from Elsie. Guess my nonchalant text wasn't as casual as I thought. Avery's call probably isn't too far behind.

"Hey..."

"Oh my god, Grace! Are you okay? I'm almost home. The stupid breakfast lasted longer than expected."

"I'm fine. Just a little beat up. Nothing rest won't cure."

"Are you sure you shouldn't go to urgent care or something?"

"Nah, I'm good." I have health insurance now, but after handling every injury on my own for so long, I can't justify a visit to the hospital unless I know I'm not fine. Like on *death's doorstep* not fine.

This doesn't qualify.

Elsie's sigh could blow over one of the trees lining our street. "So stubborn. I'll be home soon, then I'll judge for myself how *good* you are. See you in five."

Hanging up, I preemptively call Avery to fill her in as my head sinks into the back of the overstuffed chair.

What a weekend.

The Ole Aces fiasco then the bike run-in this morning.

Maybe I should've been more specific with the universe when I said I wanted change...

TO CONTINUE MY CAMPAIGN of being more social—and to avoid letting the disaster of last weekend scare me off from trying again—I message Susie, the receptionist at Casey & Sons, asking if she wants to hang out at the Apple Fest carnival tonight.

It's short notice, but I'm hoping for the best.

We've chatted a couple of times at work, and she's got a different vibe than Kayla and her group, so my fingers are crossed that I'll have better luck in the friendship department with her.

God, making friends as an adult is hard.

I feel like I'm back in freaking high school, begging for attention from anyone who will notice me.

My phone lights up with a text.

Susie: *Sorry, already have plans, but thanks for asking!*

Sighing, I put on a brave face and reply.

Me: *That's alright! I knew it was late notice but thought I'd check lol. Have fun! :)*

There. That didn't sound needy or upset. *It's not personal*, I tell myself. Her life doesn't revolve around me, and just because this time is a no-go doesn't mean future get-togethers won't happen. No big deal.

"We'll just go by ourselves."

Shadow wags his tail in excitement. Avery, Elsie, and I are going to the carnival next Saturday, but tonight's admission is free with a canned food item since it's a Monday. I figured it'd be the perfect low-risk opportunity for another socializing attempt. "We'll practice enjoying events as a single person, right, boy?"

He yips in agreement, and my mood immediately brightens.

At the carnival, Shadow and I share a funnel cake as we wander through aisles of rides, games, and food trucks. The host, Miss Patty's Orchard, has signage everywhere, and there's an apple-flavored something at all the vendor stalls. Even our funnel cake has spiced apples on top.

At first, I felt a little self-conscious—the lone woman and her dog ambling through families and groups of friends. Then it became obvious that nobody cared. They were too focused on their own enjoyment to notice me, which loosened the chains of anxiety knotted in my chest.

Pausing between two stalls for a breather from the crowds, I tell Shadow, "Last one," and toss a piece of dough into his waiting mouth before throwing the paper plate in the bin behind me.

We're about to step back into the fray when a familiar high-pitched voice drifts over the buzz of laughter and conversation surrounding us. Peering around the corner of a tent, I see Kayla, her girls, and Susie, giggling as they get in line for the Tilt-a-Whirl.

A sledgehammer demolishes the bit of confidence tonight had given me. Why is Susie here after refusing my carnival offer? Why didn't she invite me along? It's not like I'm a stranger to Kayla and her friends.

My mind races with excuses.

Maybe she wanted a girls' night without me, the new girl, especially since I spent Friday night with Kayla, Lindsey, and Brittany. Maybe her original plans fell through, and this was a last-minute decision. I can't exactly blame her for forgetting me—we haven't known each other for that long, right?

Still, feelings of rejection slick my gut.

This really is like high school again.

I never had close friends since my family moved around so much, but there would always be a couple of girls I connected with wherever we were.

One time at my second high school, we agreed to meet up at the ice rink. After waiting alone at the rink for thirty minutes, I decided it wouldn't seem too desperate to call and see where everyone was. That first conversation made it clear that no one was coming. They didn't think we'd made 'concrete plans,' so the hang out was completely forgotten.

Humiliation had washed over me after the conversation ended, and I had to call my parents to come pick me up, playing things off like everything was fine—like my poor sixteen-year-old heart wasn't aching.

Susie shifts, putting me directly in her line of sight. Afraid of being spotted, I retreat further between the stalls as Shadow whines and licks my hand. He knows something is wrong, but how to explain to a dog that the person he thinks is amazing doesn't measure up in the eyes of humans.

"Grace, is that you?"

Fuck my life.

Why does it have to be Wes catching me at such a vulnerable moment?

I inhale a deep breath to compose myself before easing out of the shadows.

"Hey..."

"Is something wrong?" His bearded jaw tightens as he searches the shadowy space over my shoulder for the reason why I'm cowering in the dark.

"I'm fine. Why?" Light and chipper. That's what I'm going to be. He doesn't need to know the sad state of my mind right now.

"You look like you're about to cry. Are you here with someone? Did he do something?" The intensity in Wes's features is bewildering. Why does he care so much? I've done nothing but lob insults or push him away because my attraction to him makes me nervous.

"No one did anything to me." At that moment, Susie and the other women come into view. Panicking because I don't want them to see me, I scramble closer to Wes, using his large body as a shield.

His hands eclipse my wrists. "Then what the hell is going on?"

Sighing, my chin drops to my chest to avoid his gaze. "I'm avoiding Kayla and her gang. I asked Susie to hang out, she said she couldn't, now she's here with them. End of story." Once the women disappear, I try slipping away from him, but his grip remains firm. Gentle, but unyielding.

"You shouldn't hide from those bitches. You need to show them they can't fuck with you."

A bubble of slightly unhinged laughter bursts free. I've never been one to incite confrontation or get revenge. Too messy for an anxious little mouse like me. "And how exactly do I do that?"

"Come on." His hold shifts to encapsulate my hand then he tugs me in the direction of the group.

"I don't think..."

"Don't think—*do*." With that nugget of wisdom, we walk until we reach the end of a food line, mere feet behind Kayla.

"This won't help my cause."

"Why not? You're out here, doing fine without them."

"Yeah, but I'm with you," I blurt out. *Crap!* There I go again, lobbing freaking insults. *What is wrong with me?* "Sorry... It's just that they really don't like you."

"The feeling is mutual. But I'm more concerned with your feelings. Do you want me to leave?" His dark eyes bore into mine.

"Aren't your friends wondering where you are?"

"I do what I want," he says simply. "Answer the question. Do you want me to leave?"

I don't know how I feel about Wes ditching his friends so cavalierly, but the tingle in my belly confirms that I'm glad he's with me. "You can stay."

I can't bring myself to meet his eyes. It's embarrassing enough admitting that I don't want to be alone, especially when I'm trying to avoid sounding needy or desperate.

But there's no denying I'm hungry for more of Wes's attention—no matter what type of woman that makes me.

CHAPTER SIX

WES

Satisfaction, warm and triumphant, settles in my gut. Grace wants me to stay despite the judgment of her so-called friends.

It's not surprising they left her out—they're selfish bitches. And while I don't like that Grace is hurt, I can't help but appreciate getting to spend time together, since our paths haven't crossed in a week.

Refusing to waste more of the night talking about Kayla and her posse, I ask, "How's your head?"

"Good, thanks. I had a small headache later that night, but nothing too terrible."

That's a relief.

I'd never admit this aloud, but my phone remained on the highest volume setting all week in case Grace needed help. The damn ringtone was a constant nuisance as it blasted through Dusty's with each and every call that *wasn't* from the woman I waited for.

Max would have a field day if he knew. He'd be pretty smug if he could see me now, too. Thankfully, he's too busy helping Kendra run the Miss Patty's Orchard booth, since Kendra is their marketing guru, and this carnival is their biggest event of the year.

That's why I'm here—they needed extra hands hauling in crates of apples. Once we finished, I was about to leave when I spotted Grace.

"I'm glad to hear your stubborn refusal to see a doctor didn't turn out badly."

"Like I knew it wouldn't."

We reach the front of the line as she finishes, and I wave off her money as a funnel cake large enough to share appears along with two frozen lemonades.

It may be a little chilly for the icy drink, but you can't go to the Apple Fest without splurging on Miss Patty's Rose Lemonades. They're a carnival staple that look and taste like strawberry lemonade but are made with the orchard's Hidden Rose Apples.

Grace grabs the warm funnel cake while I carry our drinks to an empty picnic table in a quieter corner of the grassy lot where the festival is held.

"Thanks for this, by the way." Grace holds up a bite of funnel cake. "This is our second of the night, but I'm not mad about it."

"Happy to help you exceed your sugar quota for the day." Besides, if it keeps her by my side, I'll buy as many funnel cakes as she wants. "So, what's your story?"

"What do you mean?" The words are guarded as her shoulders stiffen.

Her immediate apprehension is a surprise, and I'm not exactly the most forthcoming guy when it comes to talking about myself.

But that's me—a man used to being judged for my family and my youthful mistakes. What does Grace have to worry about?

"You don't have to share anything you're uncomfortable with," I say, hoping to put her at ease. "I just meant why did you move here? What do you do? The usual questions when getting to know someone."

"Oh, right... Of course." A scarlet blush blooms with her self-conscious laugh. "Things were stagnant back home, so I made a change. My friend Avery lives here and hooked me up with a job interview. Now, I work at Casey & Sons as a paralegal."

Fuck Casey.

That explains how she got tangled up with Kayla.

"Your turn. Tell me about Wes Gallagher, since I'm not sure how much truth was in Kayla's description," she mumbles around the straw of her lemonade.

"Absolutely zero, I bet." Dropping my hand below the table top, I let Shadow sniff my fingers before licking away the powdered sugar.

I need this guy on my side when it comes to Grace, and bribing him seems like a wise move. It's definitely better than having him growl at me like he did at the park.

"I'm a local. My mom lives in Arizona with her third husband, and my dad lives alone in the house I grew up in. I worked at Dusty's for years before the previous owner agreed to sell it to me." This is where I pause, contemplating how much to share before deciding to bite the bullet. In this town, it's impossible to keep secrets anyway.

"You've probably heard that I've been to jail."

She nods, sitting straighter on the picnic bench. Wariness enters her eyes..

I get it but still fucking hate it.

Dragging a hand through my hair, I sigh. "Contrary to the rumors, I've only been there once. For a night. The sheriff locked me up for underaged drinking and was trying to teach me a lesson..." *And boy did I learn one.* A sly grin loosens the straight line of my mouth as I recall that time in my life. "I learned to be more careful and not get caught."

Grace chuckles and shakes her head in mock disapproval. "Why do they act like you're a violent ex-convict that will act out at any moment?"

"It's a small town. Everything gets blown out of proportion. Add the fact that I was born poor white trash and started a lot of brawls growing up, you end up with me being a dangerous felon. But all of those fights were against assholes who thought they could insult me without consequence because mommy and daddy were members of the country club."

Exhibit A: Kayla Casey, formerly Kayla Rhodes.

Exhibit B: Andrew and Brandon Casey.

"I'm sorry for how they treat you." She reaches across the table to squeeze my forearm, and I wish like hell we were skin to skin rather than my stupid long-sleeved tee blocking contact.

"No need to apologize. Their behavior only matters when it affects what I want." I stare into her blue eyes, the pretty color full of empathy. Flipping my arm over, my fingertips brush along her exposed wrist. "And right now, I want to know what you're thinking. Am I an irredeemable bastard?"

Grace fidgets in her seat, her chest rising and falling with each quick breath. She wraps a curl around her finger and tugs as her teeth nibble on her bottom lip.

"No, I would never think that." The words are soft but firm. "You're a good man, Wes. You helped me out of a jam with my car, and tonight you rescued me from what was about to turn into a pity party."

"*Good* may be pushing it, considering the thoughts I've had about you, but I'll take it." Reading the question on her face, I wink. "Trust me, they're not appropriate for a family-friendly carnival."

Grace shyly ducks her head, but it's the truth, and I don't see the point in hiding the erotic dreams she's starred in. She's an attractive woman. Short. Curvy. A perfect handful.

"Um, I'll take your word for it. Do you want to walk around some more?"

"Hell, yeah. How about we swing by Miss Patty's booth? I can introduce you to Max's wife, Kendra."

We head in that direction, and at one point, Kayla sees us, her mouth gaping open like a beached fish, but Grace doesn't comment, so neither do I.

Our destination clears of guests when the family of five Kendra was talking to waves goodbye, leaving an opening for us to step up to the table.

"Well, look who decided to return. Are you planning on helping us pack up tonight, too?" Kendra asks with a raised eyebrow.

"Nope, I just wanted to introduce Grace and her dog, Shadow. They're new in town, but they're friends with Elsie Hawkins from the elementary school."

Max jumps to his feet and offers Grace a hand to shake. "We've already met, but since you had a head injury at the time..." He shrugs sheepishly. "Max Linfield, Wes's best friend since kindergarten, and this beautiful woman is my wife, Kendra. How do you know Wes? I don't think you mentioned it before."

No one could ever accuse Max of being subtle. He cuts right to the chase.

"We met on my first day in town. One of my tires blew on the drive in, and he was kind enough to take care of it for me."

"Was he now?" Max turns to me with a sly expression. The puzzle pieces are coming together for him. My fixation at The Ole Aces. Our run-in at Dusty's. The bike accident. And now meeting at the carnival.

Kendra elbows him in the gut. "Welcome to Suitor's Crossing. Have you been to the bridge yet?" The conversation continues from there as the women launch into the charm of the town's legend.

Another hour passes before Grace yawns and bows out for the evening with a promise to plan a coffee date with Kendra. We walk to the edge of the park, away from the gravel parking lot of cars, so I ask, "Did you drive?"

"No, I biked. It's locked up over there." She points to a metal rack. Hers is the lone bicycle left.

"I'm gonna have to get you on a real bike soon."

"I d-don't know... I've never been on a motorcycle."

That doesn't surprise me.

Grace is a good girl.

Riding on the back of a Harley, clinging to a man with those soft hands of hers doesn't fit that image.

"We need to change that," I rasp, tucking a stray curl behind her ear, my hand lingering on her skin. Grace's breathing hitches in her chest as her lashes flutter against her cheeks.

I'm going to kiss this woman.

I *need* to kiss this woman.

Swooping forward, our lips press together in a simple yet electric touch.

And my whole world is changed.

Because Grace is shy yet giving and so damn sweet it fucking hurts. My tongue teases her bottom lip until she allows me entry, and I groan at the slick heat of her mouth.

There's a crack in my chest. A fissure opening beneath the weight of a thousand different emotions. It's momentous. Terrifying.

All because of a kiss.

And I know I'm fucking screwed.

CHAPTER SEVEN

GRACE

A pile of dirty clothes overflows my hamper, which means it's time for one of my least favorite chores. And no matter what time I go to the laundromat, there's a crowd of people, making privacy an impossibility.

Add that to my list of requirements for a future home: a laundry room.

Thankfully, the parking lot only has two other vehicles when I arrive. Maybe I got lucky, and this is the prime time to go.

Mentally crossing my fingers, I grab a cart from inside and wheel it to my car to load up the heavy plastic hamper along with the pillows and comforter I brought.

The metal basket rattles over the concrete as I guide it toward the laundromat's front doors—manual ones rather than automatic.

Who thought requiring patrons to swing the door open while simultaneously shoving a heavy cart over the bump of the door frame was a good idea?

This really is a two-person job.

Too bad I'm a single woman, and Elsie went to her parents' for the weekend.

Someone pushes the door open from the inside.

"Thanks!" My grateful smile falters at seeing Wes holding the door for me. I haven't seen him since our impromptu kiss at the Apple Fest carnival two weeks ago—which isn't to say I haven't thought about him.

No, it seems I can't shake the man out of my head, and it doesn't help that Elsie keeps bringing him up.

She's still high from Avery taking her advice about dating Dominic and ending up freaking engaged. Now, my roommate likens herself to some sort of relationship guru, and I'm next in line for a sprinkle of her magic.

Wes grabs the other end of my cart and lifts it over the ledge like it weighs nothing. "You're welcome. I saw you coming in, so I thought I'd help."

"Excuse me." A young mother with her kid in tow stands behind Wes with a mountain of folded clothing in her cart, waiting for me to move, so she can leave.

Offering an apology to the woman, I wave to Wes before escaping to the large industrial washers in the back, preferring to toss everything into one giant machine rather than separating items out the proper way. All of my clothes run on cold anyway, and if every once in a while, I have a white cami come out pink, I'm willing to accept that consequence.

After throwing everything in, I survey my seating options. An older lady is reading a magazine at one end of the row of chairs along the wall while Wes is on his phone at the other end.

You kissed the man. Now, you're too afraid to sit by him?

Rolling my eyes at the silliness, I choose a chair one over from Wes. It gives us space but not enough to seem like I'm ignoring him.

Not that I am.

I'm just... *flustered*. Men don't kiss me out of the blue like that, especially not bearded mechanics with tattoos for days, and a penchant for coming to my rescue.

Determined to remain casual, I find my reading tablet and jump back into *Northanger Abbey* after deciding to take a break from my usual sexy romances. I needed to cleanse the palette, so to speak, by reading a classic. And Jane Austen is nothing if not a classic.

"What are you reading?"

Jolted out of Catherine and Mr. Tilney's first meeting, I glance up to find Wes studying me curiously. "*Northanger Abbey* by Jane Austen."

"Never heard of it." He shakes his head. The shaggy ends of his hair brush across his shoulders, and my fingers itch to run a hand through the thick strands.

I shrug off the inappropriate compulsion. "It doesn't get as much press as *Pride and Prejudice* or *Sense and Sensibility*." A blank look overtakes his features. "Tell me you've at least heard of *Pride and Prejudice*? Elizabeth Bennet? Mr. Darcy?"

"Nope. But I don't really read for fun. I stick to my textbooks."

Textbooks? Is he attending college while running Dusty's?

"What about English class, though? Austen seems like required reading, which would be textbook-adjacent."

Wes chuckles, showing off a glimpse of his smile. It's too bad he's getting glaring lines rather than laugh lines, because he's got a sexy laugh, deep and rumbly like a jungle cat's purr.

"I'll take your word for it. What does she write?"

I launch into an explanation about how they're romances that offer a study of social classes and themes of the time period. "The book I'm reading now is a favorite of mine along with *Pride and Prejudice*. You should watch the movie because I doubt you'll be able to sit through the six-hour miniseries," I tease.

"Six hours? Holy shit. Why don't you break it down for me?"

"You really want to hear about the antics of Elizabeth Bennet and Mr. Darcy?"

Wes raises an eyebrow, crosses his tattooed arms over his chest, and relaxes into his seat, clearly waiting for me to begin.

Okay, then.

The next twenty minutes are spent with me gushing over two of my favorite literary characters while Wes asks the occasional question.

Wrapping up, I add, "Of course, while I'd like to think of myself as Lizzie, Avery has said I'm more like Jane with Mr. Bingley."

"Why would she think that?"

My face heats at the question. I don't want to explain, but Wes waits expectantly as I try to think of how to not completely embarrass myself.

Yeah, that's impossible.

"There's this guy or used to be this guy... And she thought what was going on between us sounded like Jane and Bingley."

There. That wasn't too bad. Vague but still answered the question.

"How? Because you're the oldest like Jane?"

Geez, he's persistent.

"Um, no. More like we always kind of tiptoed around each other. Everyone else saw how much we 'belonged' together—their words not mine—and how it was going to take forever for us to get together because of how shy and reluctant we were to say how we felt."

My washer releases a piercing beep to announce the end of its cycle, saving me from more questions. "So, yeah... I'm going to put my stuff in the dryer now."

Wes looks like he's about to press for more information, but I hightail it across the tiled floor. No need to elaborate on an old crush that never culminated into anything, especially when the guy in question is now happily married with two kids.

I spy Wes dumping a load of damp clothing into another dryer and realize he must've gotten here right before me.

When my things are divided between two dryers, I shuffle back to my seat, where Wes is already waiting for my return. Clearly, he doesn't have as much crap as I do.

"So, textbooks...." *Time to turn this conversation in a different direction.* "What's that about?"

"I'm getting my degree online for business management. Figured it will benefit Dusty's."

"That's smart, though it sounds like you've got a packed schedule between running the garage and attending classes."

A plethora of unspoken questions hangs in the air. How did he inherit Dusty's? What made him decide to earn a degree so long after high school? But I keep all of those to myself.

It's none of my business, even if I'm intensely curious.

Wes scrubs the back of his neck with a sigh. "Yeah, I'm pretty busy. Sometimes I wonder if I'm wasting my time and money on classes when Dusty's is doing fine, but I kind of want the degree." A chagrined half-smile peeks through his beard.

"There's no shame in that. Just because it's not a necessity business-wise doesn't mean it's not worth something to you personally."

When the dryers stop tumbling, we fold our dried clothes on the tables next to each other. I surreptitiously stuff my underwear and bras into the hamper to avoid anyone seeing them. That's the other awkward part about using a laundromat—worrying about strangers spotting your panties.

At least Wes seems preoccupied with his own clothes.

He hefts my hamper into a laundry cart then tugs both of our carts outside while I get the doors. Without a word, he places my items in the trunk, and I can't help but revel in the comfort of having a strong man focused on easing my burden.

"Thank you for this." I gesture toward the heavy load of clothing I didn't have to break my back to move again.

"No problem. If you're not in a hurry, do you wanna get some ice cream? Fall flavors should still be available."

"Sure, where do you want to go?"

He points to a place across the street. "We can meet over there once I've unloaded these baskets."

Nodding, I hop in my car and drive the short distance to the little shop and sit at one of the outdoor tables while waiting for Wes.

It's a beautiful autumn day. Not too hot or cold. Perfect for a lazy afternoon eating a sweet treat.

Sounds like the perfect date.
But this isn't a date, right?
He did kiss you, remember?

"Hey, ready for some ice cream?" Wes jogs up to the shop door and opens it for me.

"Well, technically, it's frozen yogurt."

"What's the difference?" He grabs two cups and holds one out to me.

"Um, I actually don't know. One's soft and the other's hard?"

He laughs, his hand dropping to my lower back to gently guide me toward the metal dispensers.

"What flavor are you thinking?"

"I usually get cake batter or a comparable substitute. You?"

"It varies." We stop at the first lever with a Pumpkin Vanilla label above it. "How about we taste test them all and see where we land?" he asks.

As we fill the tiny paper cups with swirls of frozen yogurt, a few customers stare at us in dismay, but we're not being disrespectful, and Wes doesn't seem to care that we're the center of attention. His focus is on me, encouraging me to relax and have fun.

After adding toppings to our full cups, Wes pays after ignoring my protests, and we return to the table outside, where I study Wes out of the corner of my eye.

Red athletic shorts cling to sturdy thighs while a black tee conforms to his muscular chest. His jacket sleeves are pushed up to his elbows, so colorful tattoos are on full display, and I can't stop my eyes from wandering over them.

I've never seen someone up close and personal with so many tattoos. Yes, I've seen people with sleeves, or even their whole body covered, on the internet or TV, but seeing them this close is breathtaking.

Sure, they make him look badass—something he could pull off without any aid—but some of the lines are so delicate. My fingers itch to reach out and trace them.

Don't paw the man in public.

One design snakes up his neck before ending right below his ear, and that's when it becomes obvious that I've been caught ogling him as an unfamiliar expression crosses Wes's face.

Blushing, I cringe in my seat. "Sorry, I didn't mean to stare."

"Go ahead, sweetheart. I don't mind. Just be prepared for the consequences." His rumbled warning sends prickles of awareness down my body.

"What consequences?"

He leans forward until our knees touch. "When I feel those pretty blue eyes on me, it makes me want... *things*." The back of his hand drifts down my cheek, each rough knuckle caressing my skin before his thumb settles on my bottom lip.

The air hitches in my lungs as his eyes drop to my mouth. Ever so slowly, he brushes his thumb over the sensitive skin, his head bending closer until our mouths are inches apart.

Every breath mingles with mine.

Hot, and sweet from his apple pumpkin frozen yogurt.

"So fucking pretty," he murmurs.

I sway closer to him, my body suddenly lethargic. I want a repeat of our first kiss, but he keeps the distance between us, teasing me with the slow drag of his thumb over my mouth.

Emboldened, my tongue peeks out for a quick little lick, causing his eyes to darken with need as they return to mine.

"My baby wants to play?" The endearment spoken in his possessive tone shoots straight to my clenching core.

Despite the cool fall weather, sweat gathers on my skin as arousal blazes a path from my breasts to the throbbing of my clit.

Until the intense moment is broken by kids bursting through the shop door.

I jerk away from Wes, embarrassed to be caught in such an intimate position. *Holy fuck, what just happened?* I was minutes away from crawling into his lap and begging for a kiss—on a public patio where anyone could see us.

"I... I think we should probably go. My clothes need to be put away, and so do yours." I stand abruptly, the metal chair scraping against the concrete sidewalk.

"Baby... I mean... *fuck*. Grace, wait!"

Wes's truck is parked next to my car, so there's not much space between us but it could be an ocean after the intimacy of earlier.

"I'm sorry, okay? I shouldn't have... Shit, I don't know what I was doing." He reaches out before stopping himself, crossing his arms instead and causing the muscles to flex with his restraint.

"It's fine," I say, overly chipper. "But we were done eating, and I really need to get home, so..."

Please don't push this.

I don't regret what happened, but I also don't know how to process it right now. Which means putting some distance between me and Wes so I can think straight.

"Yeah, okay. I'll see you around?"

"Sure!" An awkward smile stretches my cheeks as I sink into the driver's seat.

Before exiting the parking lot, I glance in the rearview mirror. Wes has both hands on the hood of his truck, his head bowed between them, and I wonder what the hell all of this means.

CHAPTER EIGHT

WES

G race is on my mind for the rest of the night.

I shouldn't have touched her. The day had been perfect until I fucked it up by trying to put a move on her.

But catching her look of appreciation had short-circuited my self-control. I gladly would've laid back and let her gaze to her heart's content if it meant having her eyes on me.

And the temptation to see if there was more behind Grace's perusal was too much to resist, especially when I've been craving another kiss from her for weeks.

She'd seemed as drunk on the moment as me. The flush of desire on her skin couldn't be faked.

Hell, she licked me!

The brief touch had sent fire straight to my cock before everything ended as quickly as it began, and she fled like a hunted doe in the forests surrounding Suitor's Crossing.

Deciding to add salt to the wound, I search for the books we talked about at the laundromat because curiosity gnaws at my gut. I need to know more about that Bingley guy and why her friends think Grace belongs with someone like him.

Clicking on the first link for Jane Bennet, an article loads that describes a kind, intelligent, and beautiful girl.

Definitely Grace.

The author uses a similar description for Charles Bingley. Both characters are gentle personalities who see the best in people—a perfect fucking match.

I toss my phone on the couch, disappointment and frustration forming knots in my belly.

Of course, Grace would go for a man like that.

Gentle. Kind.

Fuck, even intelligent.

No one has ever used those words to describe a Gallagher, let alone me.

I'm a brute. Trailer trash. A dumb motherfucker who lazes around Dusty's.

I bet there's not a single character in Jane Austen's books that resembles me. I don't even warrant a mention on the page because I'm not a woman's dream hero.

Normally, that wouldn't concern me.

But I'm afraid Grace may be my dream girl, and we're as mismatched as they come.

CHAPTER NINE

GRACE

Elsie, Shadow, and I spend Sunday exploring the trails around the Suitor's Crossing bridge. We keep the walk slow and easy, the fresh mountain air much needed—along with our conversation about Wes.

One unexpected kiss plus an almost kiss.

What did they tally up to?

That's what we were still trying to figure out as I drove back to the apartment, theorizing aloud when the car engine stuttered to a stop in the middle of the street.

"Seriously? Not again..." I groan in disbelief. The vehicle is twelve years old and rough around the edges, but it's like all my years of good fortune have finally run out because two car problems in quick succession? Bad fucking luck.

The guy behind us blares his car horn.

"You guide the steering wheel while I push from the back. Hopefully, we can roll out of the street and to the gas station before that dude blows a gasket," Elsie says, unbuckling her seatbelt.

I nod in agreement and pop the driver's door open, keeping one hand on the wheel while pushing against the door. With both of us working together, Elsie and I manage to get my car to the oil-stained parking lot, collapsing in our seats once we're done.

Shadow braces his paws on the console and licks my cheek before I shove him back. "Not now, kid. Let me think."

There's an obvious solution to my problem, though I hesitate to bring it up.

What choice do you have?

"Should I call Wes? He might be able to help."

Elsie's eyes light up with glee. "Yes, do it! Oh my god, this is perfect!"

I roll my eyes at her enthusiasm while dialing his number, nerves pitching a tent in my belly as I wait to see if he picks up.

"Hey..." His wary tone has me rethinking the call. It's obvious my abrupt escape yesterday put him on guard.

"Hey, Wes. This is Grace." *Obviously.* My palm slaps my forehead. "Elsie and I were out, and my car just kinda died. Is there someone who can come take a look or tow it to your garage?"

Wes's tone perks up immediately, and he lets me know that he'll be twenty minutes after I give him our location. True to his word, a tow truck turns into the lot right on the dot.

"Let's see what we've got." Wes pops the hood. Worn jeans and a light blue shirt are his uniform today, both stained with oil.

It looks like he came straight from working underneath another car, and I feel bad for interrupting him when he already juggles a packed schedule.

He checks a couple of things before lifting his head. "Your spark plug wiggled loose. It should be fine now. Try it out."

The car starts without a hitch, and Wes slams the hood shut. After turning the car off, I hop out with a relieved smile. "Thanks a lot. I'm glad it was an easy fix."

"Me, too," Elsie adds before letting Shadow out of the backseat. "This guy has been prancing around like crazy. I think he needs to potty." She shoots me a mischievous grin, her eyes darting between me and Wes, as she steals my dog as a cover to leave us alone.

I don't know what she expects to happen. We're in a freaking parking lot in broad daylight.

"How much do I owe you?" I ask.

"Nothing."

"What? I can't let you work for free. It's not right."

"Tough shit. I'm not accepting a dime," he growls before tossing the rag he used to clean his hands in the cab of the truck. It doesn't look like it accomplished much, but whatever. That's the least of my concerns at the moment.

"Why?" Genuine confusion wrinkles my brow. This is his job, his business. Even though we're friends—maybe, potentially, *more* than friends—he deserves to be compensated for his time.

He hesitates then backs me into the side of his truck, so we're hidden from Elsie and the street of passing cars.

"Because you don't owe me a fucking thing. You need my help? Take it; it's free. I don't want your money." His hulking body radiates heat as his arms cage me against the warm metal of the truck. My muscles threaten to melt from the blazing inferno surrounding me—the truck, his dominant stance, the unrelenting desire in his brown eyes.

"But..."

Wes shakes his head, and his hand lightly circles my throat. "You don't get it, do you, baby? Well, let me make it crystal fucking clear."

His thumb tugs my mouth open as his lips descend on mine. His tongue sweeps inside like an invading Viking, pillaging and claiming what he wants.

Whenever we're together, the restraints around Wes seem to loosen more and more to reveal a possessive man intent on staking a claim on me. It's a heady realization as his rough beard rakes across my skin with each tilt of his head to get a deeper angle.

His calloused fingertips caress my cheek while his hips dig into mine, pinning me to the truck with the hard dick nestling between my thighs.

A low moan vibrates between us, and I can barely breathe—not because his hold on me is too tight but because of how damn erotic this is.

I'm not the girl men like Wes, tatted and dangerous, obsess over.

I'm not the woman a man like him craves.

Time loses all meaning as we stand there, kissing and groaning and touching and finally releasing the tension left over from yesterday.

Until he retreats, nipping my bottom lip one last time. "This is what I want from you. Your time, your mouth, everything. Give it to me, Gracie." The demand sends a shiver down my spine and hot arousal soaks my panties.

I struggle to fathom how I affect him so intensely, but I do. The hard bulge of his cock, his heavy breathing and hooded eyes, are proof of his desire.

I lick my lips, searching for a response, when something on my cheek catches his eye, and his entire body freezes. Jerking away, Wes mutters a line about getting back to work, then drives off, leaving me stunned.

"What happened?" Elsie asks, leading Shadow to my frozen position on the blacktop.

"I have no clue."

Maybe his feelings aren't so clear, after all...

CHAPTER TEN

WES

Once I'm back at Dusty's, I throw myself into fixing up the vehicle I'd been working on before abandoning it like my heels were on fire, itching to 'rescue' Grace.

Because I'd been excited to see her again. *Too* excited.

Which is why when her friend left us alone, I couldn't resist touching her. Tasting her sweet mouth again, teasing the shyness from her.

It took all my willpower to pull back, but once I did, the marks I left behind were obvious. The oil streaks on my hands had rubbed off onto her soft skin, revealing the reality of our differences.

She's clean, sweet, and I'm fucking dirty. *Trailer trash*, if you believed Kayla and her gang of bitches.

I don't deserve to touch Grace.

She doesn't belong in my world, and I can't forget that again.

Or else end up like my dad.

Alone because he dared to care for a woman out of his league.

"Fuck!" The clang of my wrench echoes off the concrete walls of the garage. This is why I don't do relationships. Women tie you in knots. Leave you dreaming of impossible things.

And if you give into those dreams?

There's every possibility that she'll realize her mistake and leave you in the dust the moment you finally have everything you've ever wanted.

CHAPTER ELEVEN

GRACE

Crossing's Cups & Cakes buzzes with activity, though I'm tucked far away from the front counter, chilling at a corner table with Elsie and Avery. The events of the past few weeks spilled out like a dam breaking loose, catching Avery up with everything since she's been so busy starting her new interior decorating business.

"Whoa, girl, you didn't waste time kicking your old life to the curb. I'm proud of you!" Avery pats my arm and grins, the diamond ring on her left hand sparkling under the lights.

"Same. And a little jealous. I need some of what you've got." Elsie pouts, no doubt stewing over the latest problem at the elementary school where she works. Between school politics and parent drama, it would be the prime spot for a show called *The Real Teachers of Suitor's Crossing*.

Slumping against the back of my chair, I shrug. "I don't feel like I actually did anything, though. It's more a matter of aligning coincidences, you know?"

"*Heart sparks* at work." Avery nods sagely.

"How many times do I have to walk across that damn bridge for them to start kicking in for me?" Elsie jokes, swallowing the last of her chai latte.

My phone vibrates on the table as Avery pep talks Elsie. There's a message from Wes, which immediately causes the coffee I consumed to roil around in my gut.

"Um... Wes just texted me. He wants to know if I'd like to go to a Reaper's Wolves party on Friday. What should I say?" I haven't heard from him since that awkward moment by my car when he declared his intentions then promptly ditched me.

"Yes! *Duh.* I met a couple of those guys when I worked at Design Time. They're nice. Not at all sketchy like some people think," Avery scoffs.

"But it's a biker party. They might be cool, but I'm definitely not. I'll be out of place."

"No, you won't. If Wes thinks you'll be fine, then you will be. Come on, don't fail us now. Look how far your bravery has gotten you. Hot kisses and a date with a sexy mechanic."

"I don't know if he considers this a date..."

"No way to know unless you go. And remember, you've got *heart sparks* on your side," Avery reminds me.

I'm not one hundred percent confident that's true, but my heart is definitely hopeful. After swiftly typing a reply to Wes, I set my phone down. I'm really doing this—attending a party at an MC compound.

And while I'm there, maybe I'll muster enough courage to confront Wes about this hot and cold act he's got going on.

Because I'm ready to find out if he really is my *heart spark*—if this pull between us is something more than a passing attraction—but he has to meet me halfway.

CHAPTER TWELVE

WES

G ravel crunches beneath the truck tires as I park in front of Grace's apartment. My buddy Timber invited me to a get-together at the Reaper's Wolves MC compound, and something prompted me to extend the invitation to Grace, too.

A latent masochist desire? Because surely that's what this is.

Why else would I ask Grace to hang out when I know she's not the one for me? When I've never even *wanted* a 'one' in the first place?

All week, I've kept busy with work, reminding myself that I've never had a problem forgetting a woman in the past. Why should this be any different?

But Grace is like a drug, apparently.

Because I can't shake her.

Can't get enough.

The high I feel in her presence is an addiction. Like that one Taylor Swift lyric Kendra kept singing a few months ago: "*He jokes that it's heroin but this time with an 'E.*'"

Grace is unlike anyone I've ever met, and the conversations we've had? No one else in my orbit would try to explain Jane Austen to me, and I kind of think I've been missing out because of it.

"Hey, thanks for inviting me," Grace murmurs once she's buckled into my truck.

"No problem. Figured you could use better company after dealing with Kayla." I'll pawn her off on Kendra or one of the MC guys' women.

My good deed done—knowing she's in safe hands with them—maybe I'll be able to relax and not feel this constant ache to be near her.

Twenty minutes later, we follow a cluster of people inside the warehouse converted into a communal home for Reaper's Wolves MC members. Couches and various game tables form a cozy picture, and groups of members and biker bunnies occupy the space. Spying Timber at the back of the building, I guide Grace that way for introductions.

Her steps falter a bit, and instinctively my hand rubs soothing circles over her lower back. "Relax. No one's going to bite."

The reassurance falls on deaf ears. Her face remains a little pale, while a sheen of sweat dots her forehead, and I wonder if this is a mistake. If she's this nervous to meet a couple of bikers—good guys, military veterans—then how the hell is she going to survive the rest of tonight?

"Wes, who's your friend?" Timber's dark brows scrunch together in curiosity. I usually fly solo during parties, so his bewilderment is understandable.

"This is Grace. She recently moved to Suitor's Crossing and works at Casey & Sons."

"Fuck Casey," Austin spits from his place beside Timber. He attended school with Brandon and Andrew, too, so he's well aware of their dickish behavior.

Grace jolts at the automatic rejoinder. At this point, it's instinct for us to react that way to the Casey name, but to a stranger, especially an innocent one like her, it's probably unsettling.

I make a mental note to curb the natural reaction in the future, then stop when I realize what the hell I'm doing.

What happened to never letting a woman dictate my actions?

Yet Grace didn't even say a word, and I'm already trying to change.

What the fuck?

After introductions, the conversation slips into the custom work Timber's handling at the MC-owned garage.

The entire time Grace hardly speaks. She answers questions directed her way from Lindy, the woman beside Timber, or Luna, Austin's girl, but her demeanor is a far cry from the friendly persona she had at the carnival with Max and Kendra. It's closer to the vulnerable one she had after our kiss by her car.

Maybe those oil streaks had her recognizing our differences, too.

Maybe it's finally hitting home in the midst of my friends—complete opposites of Kayla, or even Grace and her group.

"Are you okay?" I ask under my breath, squeezing her elbow as concern tightens my jaw.

"I'm fine." She drains the water bottle in her hand before grabbing another one from the cooler off to the side. She gulps that down, too.

Confused by her sudden thirst, I'm about to ask again if something is wrong when the MC president, Logan Snow, and his wife, Caroline, enter the fray. "Hey, man! Long time, no see. How have you been?"

"Good. Busy. Missing Faith."

Faith is Alaska's girl. She was the part-time receptionist for Dusty's until she went on maternity leave. That's why the waiting room is such a mess right now. She kept everything tidy and organized, but in her absence, it's gone to shit—the way it was prior to her arrival.

Probably should hire a temp until she returns.

If she returns.

It wouldn't surprise me if Faith decided to stay home with her newborn, and I wouldn't blame her. She's perfect mother material, the antithesis of my mom.

Grace taps my shoulder. "Can we leave soon?" She nervously licks her dry lips.

"Of course. Give me a minute to say goodbye." I guess forty-five minutes is her limit in a place like this, and the realization sucks.

Grace nods her head and rocks back on her heels before pausing then rushing out of the room. Worry clenches my gut as my gaze follows her hasty exit.

"I gotta go…"

The murmured farewells fade as I trail her footsteps in time to see Grace disappear into the hallway bathroom.

Debating my choices, I say, "Fuck it," and push the slightly ajar door open wider. Ragged coughing echoes off the walls. Grace is bent over the toilet, her body shuddering with each heave, and I hurry to hold her hair back as wisps of curls cling to her damp skin.

"I've got you, sweetheart. Don't worry, I'm here."

She continues to vomit until dry heaves are all that's left, then unrolls some toilet paper, wipes her mouth, and flushes everything away, leaning heavily against me as I help her stand.

More sweat shines on Grace's forehead even though shivers wrack her body. I strip off my leather jacket and drape it over her trembling frame before settling her on a chair in the kitchen—away from the crowd of people in the living area.

"I'll be right back. I'm going to grab another water bottle for you and let Timber know what's going on. Will you be alright for a few minutes?" I hate leaving her alone, but I plan on being quick.

There's a short groan in response.

When I return two minutes later, a man is kneeling in front of Grace.

"What are you doing?" I bark, marching toward the stranger hanging so close to my girl.

The guy stands and lifts his hands in surrender. "I'm just checking on her. I noticed she looked pale. Thought I could help."

"She's fine."

She's mine.

I glare at the man until he takes the hint and backs off, sparing one more glance toward Grace before leaving. Slipping my arms beneath Grace's thighs and across her back, I carry her out to my truck and carefully buckle her in. Her breathing is labored as I offer the water bottle with the cap off.

"Here, baby, sip this." This may be a twenty-four-hour stomach bug, but that doesn't mean my own belly isn't in knots worried about her.

Because I hate seeing Grace in pain.

She has to be okay.

The street that leads to her place passes on our left as I opt instead to take her to my home where I can look after her. Sure, it's still in the middle of a renovation, but I'm not abandoning my girl.

Thankfully, the drive doesn't take long, and soon, we're through the front door headed straight to my bedroom. My intentions are to get her changed into something dry—not damp with sweat—but her fingers stop me from tugging at her clothes once I set her down.

"I can do it... I need a shower." Each sentence takes longer than usual as she sways on her feet.

"I'm not sure that's a good idea."

"I'll be fine." The words sound painful coming from her raw throat, so I decide not to fight her, which will hopefully speed up the process of getting her to bed.

"Keep the door unlocked. I want to be able to get to you if anything happens."

Nodding, she shuffles into the bathroom after I give her a tee and a pair of sweatpants to wear.

Unsure of what to do while she showers, I search my drawers and cabinets for medicine. There's a purple syrup that says it helps fevers, but everything else is for coughs and sniffling.

If only it was just a cold.

It would've saved Grace a hard time puking her guts out.

I look around trying to figure out what else would be useful. A glass of water. The medicine. They both go on the nightstand, then I change into pajama pants and sit at the edge of my bed, waiting for Grace to come out again.

CHAPTER THIRTEEN

GRACE

I slowly undress before hobbling into Wes's shower. Uncontrollable chills attack my body—my teeth chattering nonstop—as I fiddle with the metal knobs. A blast of icy water smacks my face, and I jerk back and cough from the unwelcome assault.

Sleep is calling my name, but my hazy mind urges me to get clean first, so I reluctantly shift forward as the water warms. Washing is probably a good idea. I threw up earlier, and I keep sweating and shivering.

Sweating and shivering.

That's kind of fun to say, I think, as it repeats over and over in a catchy jingle. Steam billows in the glass stall, fogging the tile and adding to the weird floating feeling settling in my bones.

Mmm... This was a genius idea.

I mentally pat my back then actually pat my back with a hand to my shoulder. *Oh, wait.* I'm supposed to wash while I'm here.

Squinting, I take stock of Wes's bath products. Only male things here. Now, I'll smell like a man.

I frown.

Then another brilliant thought pops free.

I'll smell like Wes, my favorite *man.*

A giggle bubbles up at my sudden great fortune as I start with his shampoo and conditioner. Two in one. So easy for guys.

Sweating and shivering.

Sweating and shivering.

The jingle continues to play. It'd probably earn me big bucks if I sold it to a pharmaceutical company.

Imagining a bank account full of cash after selling the rights to my hit melody, I turn off the water and step out to grab a towel and dry off. The bathroom smells heavenly as Wes's shirt slides down my torso. The hem hugs my wide hips as do the sweatpants, although the length drags on the floor under my heels.

"Are you feeling any better?" Wes stands to help me to his bed once I reenter the bedroom, and I use the opportunity to lean into his sturdy warmth, his broad body a pillar of strength and stability in my weakened state.

"Drink this. It should help." He pours some liquid in a tiny plastic cup and holds it out to me. My nose wrinkles at the smell, but I choke it down.

"Good girl," Wes praises as he gently urges me under the forest green comforter on his bed, and I beam at his approval.

Good girl.

Good girl.

I think I found my second hit jingle.

Unfortunately, the goldmine song withers away as soon as my head touches the pillow, my mind and body finally succumbing to exhaustion.

CHAPTER FOURTEEN

WES

G race is out like a light as soon as she lays down.

Thankful she has a reprieve from feeling so shitty, I grab my comb from the bathroom counter then return to gently untangle her hair while it's still wet, treading lightly so as not to wake her.

The slow motion of dragging thin bristles through damp, starting-to-curl strands is a little hypnotic. And a lot soothing. The tension in my muscles drains away with each downward stroke.

Thank fuck my bedroom and bathroom are fully renovated.

I wasn't thinking clearly about bringing her to my fixer-upper of a house. It's a mess of tools and supplies—not exactly a safe haven for a sick woman—but I couldn't leave her unattended at home.

You're forgetting she has a roommate.

Ignoring the reminder, I reluctantly set the comb aside and snag my laptop to finish the homework due Monday, remaining beside Grace in case she needs anything.

Only a few more credits, and I'll be able to graduate with my bachelor's degree in business. The first Gallagher to achieve such a thing.

A light from under the bathroom door wakes me up a few hours later, retching sounds filtering through the closed door.

Grace.

Rolling to my feet, I hurry to check on her, but by the time I'm halfway through the door, she's done, spitting water into the sink.

"Hey, sweetheart. It must be time for more medicine, huh?" I'm not entirely sure it's doing anything, but even a placebo effect would be beneficial.

The purple liquid sloshes into the cup, and I offer it to Grace, who groans before shooting it back, her head tilted toward the ceiling.

With one task complete, I carefully grasp her hips and lift her onto the bathroom counter. Wetting a cloth with cool water, I wash her flushed face, the mottled skin covered in sweat and tears.

I hate seeing her like this.

There's nothing more I can do for her, and it's damn frustrating.

Grace rests her head against the wall as I continue to wipe away the evidence of her sick episode. Another shiver trembles through her limbs.

Tucking her back under the covers after finishing in the bathroom, I climb in behind her, tenderly sliding the dried curls out of her face and massaging the back of her neck with my fingers.

Eventually, sleep claims her again, and I breathe a sigh of relief.

Tired myself, I secure Grace as close as I can with my arm around her waist. My head rests in the crook of her shoulder, and each time I inhale, her natural scent mixed with my soap calms me until I, too, drift away in an ocean of dreams.

A deep ocean that I fear represents how deeply I've fallen for the woman in my arms. Because despite my best efforts, Grace slipped beneath my defenses.

And I'm clueless as to what this means for the future.

CHAPTER FIFTEEN

GRACE

S unlight pours onto my face as my surroundings come into focus.

There's a blanket tucked underneath me, along with Wes's arm and leg protectively wrapped around my body. I'm pulled tight to him like a butterfly snug in its cocoon, and my eyes flutter shut to revel in the sensation.

I feel safe.

Like nothing can hurt me while under his protection.

My relaxed state doesn't last long, though, when all the water from yesterday catches up to me, and my bladder screams for relief.

Shouldn't I be dehydrated?

I try not to wake Wes, but he tenses around me while I'm extracting myself.

"Are you feeling sick again?"

"No, just have to pee," I say, slightly embarrassed despite it being a completely normal human function.

His arm lifts to let me go, but as soon as I return, he raises the cover and rumbles, "Come back to bed."

Wes's sleep roughened voice twines around my heart, and instinctively, I obey his command, carefully situating myself while he resumes his slumber behind me. His arm and leg sneak back around my body, but I don't mind.

We still need to have a conversation about what exactly we are to each other, but that can wait. I'm too content with what we are *right now*.

WHEN I WAKE UP AGAIN, Wes is gone.

Sitting up with a yawn, my curious gaze travels around his room. He doesn't have much. A lone bed, dresser, and nightstand fill the master bedroom. No pictures or plants. Nothing personal.

Wes saunters into the room as I cover another yawn, and the sight of his tattooed body in gray sweatpants and a T-shirt really shouldn't be such a turn-on.

At least not after a horrendous night of being sick.

"You're awake. How do you feel?"

"Better."

"Good. I'll bring you a piece of toast and some juice. We'll see how you handle it," he says before retreating.

Not wanting to be away from him, I gather his pillow and blanket then carry them to the living room couch with me. The space is half-complete by the looks of the carpet partially pulled up at one corner and different patches of paint on one wall.

"What are you doing?" The demanding tone snaps me out of my perusal of the work in progress.

"I want to stay warm, and your couch doesn't have any pillows." *Sadly.* I'll have to get some for him, because how comfortable could a couch be without throw pillows?

Buying things for a man's house is serious. You're still on the fence about his feelings, remember?

"You belong in bed. I would've brought breakfast to you." Wes shakes his head and brings a small plate with two pieces of toast and a little glass filled with orange juice to my spot on the couch.

He steps over an open toolbox. "Sorry for the mess. I'm in the middle of a long renovation."

He sits beside me and flips on the television, switching channels until Saturday morning cartoons appear on the screen.

I finish half of my breakfast, afraid to eat more even though my stomach has lost that nauseous feeling. I must've had a weird twelve-hour bug or maybe ate something weird to suddenly get sick last night.

Just my luck.

Everyone seemed friendly at the MC compound, and I wouldn't have minded getting to know Luna, Lindy, and Caroline better.

Too bad my stomach had other plans.

After breakfast, sleep must claim me again, because when I wake up, I'm laid out on the couch with my legs in Wes's lap. I try pulling them back, but he stops me with a firm grip on my ankle.

"It's fine. Now, you're not so scrunched up over there." His calloused palm strokes my leg absentmindedly as he continues to watch the television screen.

"I haven't shaved."

His concentration remains on the animated show. "Don't care."

"Well, good..." I mumble, confused and a little embarrassed. Although, he handled me vomiting multiple times, so a few hairy legs shouldn't deter him.

We veg out to cartoons until the channel switches to a football game. Wes turns to me with a brow raised. "Do you want to watch this?"

When I shake my head, he flips to a movie, and I laugh at his choice.

"*Cars*?"

He shrugs sheepishly. "It's a good movie."

Okay, that's really sweet.

I tease him until the credits roll, and he tugs me further down the couch until I'm flat on my back, exposed for his tickling fingers. I playfully fight him off without success, my laughter ringing through the air.

Suddenly, Wes stops, poised over me, heat eclipsing the humor in his eyes. "I fucking love your laugh."

My breath hitches as I drag some much needed oxygen into my lungs. His body settles into mine, his hard cock nestling between my thighs perfectly.

"Wes... I need to know what this is. Before one of us runs off again."

Because it occurs to me that I've also given mixed signals. Jetting off after our first kiss. Scampering away after our impromptu ice cream date.

Wes isn't the only one to blame for our situation, but I also won't let it go much further without knowing what he's thinking.

What he's feeling.

He groans then collapses to the side of the couch, anchoring me to his body so I don't roll off the cushions.

"Damn if I know, Grace."

That's not exactly the answer I was hoping for.

"What do you mean? It's a simple question. Am I a casual hook-up or—" His hand covers my mouth to stop my nervous rambling.

"There's nothing casual about what I feel for you, and that's the problem." He scrapes a hand over his beard with a sigh.

"I don't understand."

"You're too good for me. If you're Jane, then I'm fucking Wickham—the no-good womanizer."

His reference to *Pride and Prejudice* distracts me for a second. Did he go and read the book after our discussion? Because that would be incredibly endearing.

"Wes—"

"No, let me get this out. Please." His thumb sweeps over my lips in a move reminiscent of the intimacy we shared at the ice cream shop. "I've never been interested in serious relationships. I enjoy being wild and free, answering to no one—especially a woman. My dad made that mistake. Married my mom but couldn't change who he was, a man bent on being a rolling stone. Add in the fact that the only connection they had was physical, and it was a recipe for disaster."

"That's why this thing between us shouldn't happen. There's chemistry, obviously." Wes plucks at my peaked nipple beneath his shirt. "But despite what the legend of *heart sparks* would have people believe, sparks eventually fizzle out to nothing but ash."

Damn. My heart breaks for what he's been through, but it shouldn't keep us apart. I learned that lesson the hard way—living a stunted life because of my family's issues.

"First of all, you are not your parents. If every child was forced to repeat their parents' mistakes, then I'd be in a loveless marriage with four kids and struggling to make ends meet with the measly checks I get from disability. I understand the fear of ending up like your mom and dad, trust me. That worry has held me back for more years than I care to admit. It's only recently that I'm finally breaking free from that toxic cycle, which is how I know you can do the same."

I wiggle from underneath Wes's arm to face him directly because he needs to hear this.

Hear it and *believe* it.

"There's nothing wrong with being wild and free. I want that, too. But it doesn't have to mean no strings attached. Why can't we be free together? Free to be ourselves and accept each other without conditions? I'm not too good for you, Wes. I'm just a woman doing her best to live a life worth living, and I think you're trying your best to do the same thing. Isn't it worth the risk of finding out if our best lives include each other?"

I'm not sure if it's all the self-help books and podcasts I've consumed or the work of Suitor's Crossing's *heart sparks* at play, but there's an audience of one cheering me on from inside my head.

Yes, girl, tell him!

Damn, when did you get so wise?

Wes's response will determine whether it actually has any effect, but whatever his reaction, I'm still proud of how calmly and bravely I voiced my opinion, my hope for our future. I've never done that before with anything.

A chuckle isn't what I expected.

It starts small then grows until his chest vibrates with the sound, tingling along my breasts and making my thighs rub together for relief. He may love my laughter, but his is sex personified.

Deep. Raspy. Teasing.

"Glad you find me so amusing," I huff, annoyed with my body's reaction when we're having a serious conversation.

Wes sobers and cups my cheek. "Sorry, I'm not laughing at you or what you said. It's just that you kind of proved my point by being so smart and telling me to pull my head out of my ass in the politest way possible."

Well, when he puts it that way...

A tentative grin loosens my pinched mouth. "Does that mean you're going to listen to me? Or do I need to be less polite about what I want?"

"Baby, you couldn't be anything less than who you are, no matter how hard you tried, but you've given me a lot to think about."

He scoots down the couch to rest his head on my round stomach, inhaling loudly before releasing it in a rush. "I don't want to talk about this anymore." As if to punctuate his statement, he brushes his lips over my cotton-covered belly button.

"Okay." Because I'm done talking, too. I want more of his kisses. More of what Wes has only hinted at giving me in the past.

"Okay?" he asks, glancing up to figure out how certain I am.

Nodding, my fingers dive into his hair to drag him upward until our mouths are even with each other. I lick my lips, and Wes's gaze hones in on the spot like an eagle spotting its prey from a mile away.

That's me, the little mouse offering herself up to a dangerous predator, eager to be devoured by the fire in his eyes.

CHAPTER SIXTEEN

WES

G race made solid points.

And frankly, my dick agrees with every single one.

My mind? Well, I've decided to shut it off and enjoy the moment, because I've finally got Grace's beautiful curves pressed against me, begging for the attention I'm desperate to give.

My hands slip beneath her shirt to shape the softness of her belly before sliding higher. Her budded nipples have been poking through the thin fabric, taunting me this entire time, so it's only fair that I return the favor, rolling them between my fingertips.

Grace's hips buck beneath mine. "Wes!"

"God, I love it when you say my name," I growl, lapping at her shiny lips with my tongue then dropping lower to suckle her lush breast through the cotton tee. I switch to her other nipple, leaving a dark wet circle behind.

Unerringly, one hand shifts to lightly circle her throat, and the breathy moan she releases has my cock grinding deeper into her pussy.

My name becomes a repetitive melody as I claim her body as my own, driving her closer to satisfaction with each brush of my lips, each caress of my hand.

"Give it to me, baby. Let me hear how sweetly a pretty girl like you can come for a man like me. I'm too rough and dirty for my innocent little Gracie. I knew that the moment we met. Knew it when I left those marks on your skin. Remember those, sweetheart?"

She shudders in my arms.

So close.

My breath tickles her ear, the new position putting more pressure on my hold on her neck. Not enough to hurt her—I'd never hurt my girl—but just enough to send another shiver of arousal down her gorgeous body to soak my cock.

Despite the layers of sweatpants between us, Grace is so hot, so wet, I can see the damp spot her cunt's made. See it spreading with each forceful rock of my hips as I grind my cock over her clit.

"Wes..." She claws at my back, and I relish the pain, continuing to dirty talk my girl over the edge until her cries of pleasure ring in my ears.

Along with something else.

A knock.

A fucking knock to burst our bubble.

Someone persistently bangs on the front door as if they're an escaped convict searching for asylum.

I ignore it at first, refusing to cut Grace's orgasm short, but the nuisance won't go away. Cursing under my breath, I cover Grace with the blanket then stomp across the living room to answer the door.

Alex stands on the doorstep, fist raised to knock again.

"What the fuck do you want?" I shut the door behind me as I step onto the porch. There's no way in hell I'm giving him a chance of seeing my girl so soft and sated. So vulnerable. Especially not after catching him flirting with her that first day she came into Dusty's.

"Sorry, man. I accidentally lost my key to the garage, and I'm supposed to open it tomorrow. Do you have a spare I can use?"

"Are you fucking kidding me?" This isn't the first time Alex has misplaced something important or fucked up on the job.

This is why I shouldn't have hired him.

As his friend, I knew what he was like, but I felt bad for the guy and thought I'd give him a shot.

It's bitten me in the ass more times than I can count.

And enough is enough.

CHAPTER SEVENTEEN

GRACE

"Hey, how was your weekend?" Susie waits for the Keurig to fill her mug with coffee while I toss my empty creamer bottle in the recycling bin.

"Good. Yours?"

After Wes stepped outside to deal with Alex, I quickly got dressed to go home. I didn't regret what we did, but my poor head and heart had reached their limits.

An evening of being sick followed by a cozy morning and afternoon with Wes—one that ended with a mind-blowing orgasm—had wiped the last of my reserves, and I needed some alone time to process everything.

"Same. Ran errands and squeezed in some time at the gym," she says, dumping a packet of sugar into the finished brew.

It's difficult to avoid small talk when we work together, so we've chatted a few times since the Apple Fest incident. She even apologized for what happened, explaining how her original plans fell through then Kayla invited her out.

It hadn't occurred to her to ask if I was still available until she saw me with Wes at the carnival.

I'd accepted her apology but kept a professional distance—distrust a hard thing to shake when combined with my past friendship trauma.

Besides, Elsie and Avery reminded me that it's probably smarter to keep our relationship restricted to work, anyway. No need to create an awkward situation at the place I'll be frequenting eight hours a day.

I have enough of that with Kayla stopping by every so often to visit Brandon.

On the way back to my desk, the door to Casey & Sons opens to reveal Wes striding inside the lobby. My feet automatically redirect towards him like a carrier pigeon heading home to roost.

"Morning, sweetheart." A somewhat shy grin flashes my way, and I'm taken aback by the sweetness of it.

Wes isn't shy.

Yet there's an air of uncertainty clinging to him.

Is he about to go cold on me again?

Let me down easy after the intimacy of yesterday?

"Good morning..." I drawl, suddenly nervous and curbing my initial excitement at his visit.

His grin fades as worry bunches his brows. "Is everything alright?"

Susie settles behind the reception desk, cutting off my response. I don't want her witnessing this. No doubt she'll report back to Kayla.

Not that her opinion matters to me as much anymore, but I'd rather not be her next topic of gossip.

Wes must not want to be either because he gently takes my wrist and guides me outside for privacy.

"What's going on? That was one of the women with Kayla at Apple Fest. Did something happen?"

His hands rub up and down my arms in a soothing pattern. Surely, he wouldn't be so concerned if he's about to end whatever this is between us, right?

"This isn't about Susie," I say. "Why are you here? Do you have an appointment?"

"No, I came to see you. I had a bit of a rough morning and needed a pick-me-up." His shaggy hair becomes more disheveled with the shake of his head. "Sorry, this was a stupid idea. I don't usually—"

"Stop." I cover his mouth with my palm. "I'm sorry for being weird. You just seemed a little awkward inside—an anomaly from what I know about you—so I was worried you were about to push me away again. Tell me what happened this morning."

Wes frowns and wraps his fingers around the back of my neck to tug me closer. Our mouths are inches apart, and I can't see anything but the darkness in his eyes.

"For the record, I'm done with that bullshit, Grace. I'm in this until you decide otherwise, and even then, I won't let go without a fight."

"Oh." That sounds... perfect. Amazing. Panty-dropping hot. Swallowing past the lump in my throat, I nod in understanding. "Okay. Um... me, too."

"Good." A hard kiss punctuates the word of satisfaction before his mouth drifts lower, his face burying itself in the groove between my neck and shoulder as a heavy sigh warms my skin. "I fired Alex this morning."

"What? Why?"

"Yesterday was the last straw. That on top of things like mistakes and his attitude made it obvious it was time to let him go, even if he is my friend. Or was. Not sure our friendship will continue after this. I almost let him go yesterday but didn't want to get into an argument while you were waiting for me inside."

"You made the right decision," I whisper in his ear. "Firing him in your office is more professional than doing it on your porch, though I'm sorry you had to do it at all."

"Thanks. It's definitely a lesson learned. One of my professors warned against mixing friendships with business. I should have listened to her. Won't make that mistake again."

He squeezes me in a big bear hug as if I'm the one in need of comfort rather than him. Returning the favor, my arms circle his trim waist and give as good as I got, causing Wes to grunt then laugh at my feeble attempt to match his strength.

"God, I needed that." He pauses then admits, low and passionate, "Need you."

Those two words disarm me.

They're dangerous—can cause a girl to fall in love without even realizing it.

Don't pretend like you're not already halfway in love with the man.

CHAPTER EIGHTEEN

WES

"Did you enjoy today?" We're parked at Dusty's where Grace met me before our drive to Kendra and Max's house for Thanksgiving.

I would have picked her up from her apartment, but there was a last-minute emergency with a family driving to Everton. They'd needed a quick tow and battery replacement before continuing their journey, and I couldn't *not* help them, especially on a holiday.

"I've never laughed so hard in my life. And that's saying something, because Elsie, Avery, and I have had some crazy funny conversations." Grace smiles as I help her down from my truck. "I like your friends."

"I'm glad, baby. They like you, too." I press a light kiss to her mouth, but what's meant to be brief and affectionate turns deep and desperate when her nails dig into my shoulders, pulling me closer rather than letting me retreat.

"Gracie, what are you doing to me?" I groan and bury my hands in her soft curls. The spice of pumpkin pie on her tongue is a damn delicious aphrodisiac, and I can't get enough.

Sidestepping toward the front of my truck and away from the view of the street, the only thought in my mind is claiming my girl.

Trailing kisses down her neck, I ask, "How'd you know this was a fantasy of mine?"

"Kissing me?" She laughs. "This isn't exactly the first time it's happened."

"Kissing you against my truck. That's the fantasy. Well... That's not exactly right. My fantasy is eating your pussy while your back is flat against the hood, your thighs pinned to the metal wide enough for me to fit between them."

"Hmm... who am I to deny you?" Grace eases backward, daring me to make the next move.

"Are you sure? It's dark, and everyone should be home chilling with their Thanksgiving dinner and a football game, but we're still outside. Technically, someone's headlights could light us up from the road."

Grace unzips her jacket then tosses it on the windshield. "I'm willing to risk it if you are. I'm all about taking chances these days, didn't you know?"

Thank fuck for that. Because it means she took a chance on me.

My hands grab her hips and heft her onto the hood, so she's at the perfect height for my mouth. Her legs fall open, the warm knit of her dress sliding to reveal pale thighs and lacy panties.

"God, you're beautiful. I can't believe you're mine." I bend forward and lick a line up her inner thigh, intoxicated by the scent of her arousal.

While the sun set hours ago, cool moonlight dances upon her skin, creating enticing shadows in the valley of her curves. "You won't regret giving me a chance, sweetheart."

"I know, Wes." Her palm cups the back of my head and massages my scalp. "No matter what the future holds, I'm in this. I'm tired of holding myself back out of fear. The fear of regret is finally greater than my fear of getting hurt, so I'm saying yes to you, to whatever comes next. Because you're worth the risk."

My sweet, sweet girl. Full of innocence and hope.

I vow to keep her safe. To protect her light from the cruelties of the world. From the bitchy Kaylas to the drama of her family. I want what's best for Grace, and while I may not be the best man, I'm the best man for her.

Because her happiness is my priority now.

I drag her panties off before inhaling deeply, my face nuzzled between her slick folds. "You smell so good, baby. I bet you taste even better."

Eager to confirm the suspicion, I circle her clit with my tongue then dip lower to plunge into her clenching cunt. An erotic squelch rises from the spot, and one hand drops to squeeze my dick before it explodes at the sound of how soaking wet she is.

Grace whimpers my name.

I go to work licking and sucking my girl's sweet pussy until a warm gush of arousal covers my lips and beard. Grace's body arches from the orgasm, and I don't waste time unbuttoning my jeans and finding the spare condom in my wallet.

"Grace, baby." I hold the silver wrapper to the moonlight. "This doesn't have to go further, but if you want it to, nothing would make me happier than fucking your sweet cunt until its coming around my cock. What do you say, sweetheart? You want my thick cock stretching this pussy?" I cup her between the thighs and rub my palm over her swollen clit.

"Yes... please, Wes... Don't stop," she begs. She sits up and tugs me in for a kiss, moaning as she sucks the taste of her pussy from my tongue.

Rolling the condom over my dick, I pull her lower, loving how soft and lush her body is, perfect for holding on to while I deliver on my promise to fuck these sweet curves into oblivion.

"Ready, baby?"

Grace nods, leaning back on her elbows for leverage as she lifts her hips in a silent plea. Heeding her request, I notch the head of my cock at her entrance then slowly ease inside, gritting my teeth at the tight fit.

"Fuck..." A growl of satisfaction rumbles in my throat the deeper I slide. This is the best damn cunt I've ever had wrapped around my dick, and we've barely even started.

I retreat then thrust forward. Retreat then forward. Each long plunge drags across her clit before hitting the sensitive spot inside her pussy that has Grace moaning and muttering indecipherable pleas.

I'm not going to last long this way.

Grace is too damn sexy. Too damn hot and wet and fucking perfect.

"Touch yourself, baby. Play with those heavy tits. Show me how hard you pinch your puffy nipples," I say, remembering the way they responded to my mouth when I sucked on them through her tee that day at my house.

"Oh, god... Wes..." Her nimble fingers slip beneath the vee of her neckline to pull her breasts out until they're propped up by her bra, the pink nipples standing proudly at attention atop the round globes.

Immediately, she plucks at them, and I'm mesmerized by the way they bounce with each thrust of my cock into her pussy. Her whole body jiggles from the force of our fucking—it's an addicting sight, one I plan to relive in the brightness of day where every hill and valley is visible to my hungry eyes.

"Damn, that's the sexiest thing I've ever seen, baby. You're such a good girl for me. Pinching those pretty nipples, squeezing my cock with this tight cunt. You trying to ruin me, sweetheart? Because I've never had anything this good, and I never will again. You're it for me, Gracie."

The raspy admission sends her over the edge with a cry of relief, and I quickly follow her, roaring out my orgasm as jets of cum fill the condom.

One of these days I'll fill her pussy with my seed. I'll have her walking around Suitor's Crossing dripping of me, and the thought has another shudder of pleasure tingling down my spine.

"We're gonna have to do that again," Grace murmurs once we've caught our breath.

Laughing at the breathless wonder in her voice, I pull out and ease her feet back to the ground. "Don't worry. Now that you're mine, I plan on being inside you as often as possible."

"The old me would be so jealous if she knew what was in store. You don't know how many times I dreamt of meeting a man who put me first. Who took care of me, made sure I was okay." Grace sinks into my chest and hugs my waist. "Thank you for showing me that those weren't pipe dreams. That I wasn't stupid to hope."

"You don't have to thank me for treating you the way you deserve. I'm sorry that hasn't been your experience in life so far, but we're changing our stories, remember? I'm letting down the walls I built because of my mom, and you're distancing yourself from your family to create a more loving support system."

My mom actually left a message this morning to see if I was coming home for the holiday. I texted her a 'no' then called Jordan. He understood my reasons for avoiding her and was content with our chat, letting me know he'd be playing video games all day with a buddy of his anyway.

"You're right." Grace stares up at me with a grin. "We're changing our stories for the better."

For the better.

Sounds good to me.

EPILOGUE

GRACE

Not for nothing, Suitor's Crossing may be the best town in America. It's adorable and quaint with its local shops and friendly citizens. Nature is at your fingertips with mountains rising on the horizon.

And, oh, yeah, it's got a magical legend about soul mates.

You can't get much better than that.

Especially when I met my *heart spark* the very first day I arrived in town.

The wind buffets across my body as we wind through the mountains. After a fifteen-minute lecture on safety, Wes is finally giving me that motorcycle ride he promised at the carnival.

No surprise that I love it.

The rush of adrenaline. The blast of invigorating air as we cruise down the open road. It's everything I ever dreamed of.

Wes is everything I ever dreamed of, and more.

We're wild and free together, just like I told him we could be.

And as we cross the replica of the famous Suitor's Crossing bridge, the one that welcomes visitors to our town, a laugh of pure joy bursts from my chest.

Happy and in love with my *heart spark*.

Life doesn't get much better than this.

THANKS FOR READING & DON'T FORGET TO RATE/ REVIEW!

Please consider leaving a rating/review. Ratings & reviews are the #1 way to support an indie author like me.
The more reviews, the more my books are shown to other potential readers!
And they serve as guides to readers on whether or not to take a chance on an indie author.
I appreciate your support!
XO, Hallie

ABOUT THE AUTHOR

Hallie prefers steamy, insta-love stories where curvy girls are claimed by filthy-talking heroes. And when she ran out of reading material, she decided to write her own stories. If you want a quick, hot read, she's your girl!

Don't miss out on Hallie Bennett updates by joining her VIPs here[1]!

---

1. https://www.thearrowedheart.com/hallie-bennett

www.ingramcontent.com/pod-product-compliance
Lightning Source LLC
Chambersburg PA
CBHW030353180626
46812CB00007B/2864